"Kevin Isn't Your Son?"

Hannah shook her head at Jordan's question. "I assumed everyone knew. My sister, Marybeth, died shortly after he was born."

She watched Jordan's face with growing alarm. Something was obviously wrong. "Why is it so surprising to you that Kevin is my sister's child? Did you think he was biologically mine?"

If he thought Kevin was hers, why had he never asked about Kevin's father?

"Oh…" she said softly. "Oh. You thought…"

"How could I *not* think that? The timing was right, and you seemed so…angry to see me again. And so protective of Kevin."

It all made sense to her now. Horrible, painful sense.

Jordan had wanted to be with his son.

Not *her.* But the *son* he thought he had fathered.

And now that he knew the truth…

Dear Reader,

This month we have some special treats in store for you, beginning with *Nobody's Princess,* another terrific MAN OF THE MONTH from award-winning writer Jennifer Greene. Our heroine believes she's just another run-of-the-mill kind of gal…but naturally our hero knows better. And he sets out to prove to her that he is her handsome prince…and she is his princess!

Joan Elliott Pickart's irresistible Bishop brothers are back in *Texas Glory,* the next installment of her FAMILY MEN series. And Amy Fetzer brings us her first contemporary romance, a romantic romp concerning parenthood—with a twist—in *Anybody's Dad.* Peggy Moreland's heroes are always something special, as you'll see in *A Little Texas Two-Step,* the latest in her TROUBLE IN TEXAS series.

And if you're looking for fun and frolic—and a high dose of sensuality—don't miss Patty Salier's latest, *The Honeymoon House.* If emotional and dramatic is more your cup of tea, then you'll love Kelly Jamison's *Unexpected Father.*

As always, there is something for everyone here at Silhouette Desire, where you'll find the very best contemporary romance.

Enjoy!

Lucia Macro

Senior Editor

Please address questions and book requests to:
Silhouette Reader Service
U.S.: 3010 Walden Ave., P.O. Box 1325, Buffalo, NY 14269
Canadian: P.O. Box 609, Fort Erie, Ont. L2A 5X3

KELLY JAMISON
UNEXPECTED FATHER

SILHOUETTE *Desire*®

Published by Silhouette Books

America's Publisher of Contemporary Romance

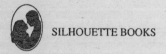 SILHOUETTE BOOKS

ISBN 0-373-76092-2

UNEXPECTED FATHER

KELLY JAMISON

began her writing career in sixth grade when she discovered that the weekly spelling assignment—to write a story using all the words on that week's list—was more fun than recess. It continued to be fun, and hard work, from then on...from the humorous greeting cards she wrote on a freelance basis to the confession stories that scandalized her mother-in-law to the romances she first published under the pen name Kelly Adams.

Along the way she wrote for two newspapers—one so strapped for cash that reporters also had to borrow a camera from the woman next door for news photos.

Kelly says she has all the ingredients for a happy life—her husband, a word processor, a nearby bookstore and a good supply of chocolate. She is always glad to hear from readers and can be reached at P.O. Box 5223, Quincy, Illinois 62305.

One

Hannah Brewster sat on the grass scowling at the two pickup trucks pulling into the driveway, her hands clenched on the shortened two-by-four lying across her lap. Just the name McClennon was enough to make her blood boil, and here came two of them now.

But these were the two older brothers, John and Jake, not Jordan McClennon, whose memory was still an aching bruise to her pride.

Hannah wouldn't have come all the way from St. Louis today if she'd known any McClennons would be here, as well, but Ronnie Wardlow had neglected to mention that little detail until a few minutes ago. On purpose, she suspected.

Ronnie had invited her to help him and some friends build a new house for his mother, Esther. Hannah liked Ronnie and his mother, and she had jumped at the chance to get out of St. Louis and into the country air at Sandford,

Illinois, on a sunny, early-May weekend. The whole plan had sounded fine until now.

The trucks drew to a stop beside Ronnie's battered pickup, and two tall, dark men got out of the vehicle. McClennons, she was sure. They were certainly a good-looking family.

The second truck had a camper top on the back, and the driver stood behind it for a couple of minutes, adjusting something with the help of the McClennon brothers. When he stepped around the pickup into Hannah's view, her heart leapt to her throat.

Jordan McClennon.

She started to stand up, then abruptly sat down again. She looked around in agitation, finally focusing on Ronnie. He gave her a helpless shrug.

Ronnie knew that she didn't like Jordan, but he didn't know the whole story.

It wouldn't have mattered much to any other woman, she supposed—a man dumping a girl after two dates was hardly headline news—but she had been young and in love. For months that love had been secret—and totally one-sided—but then one red-letter day Jordan McClennon, founder and owner of McClennon Industries in St. Louis and Hannah's employer, had bumped into her in the employees' lounge and invited her to dinner.

Hannah had never considered herself attractive; at the time she'd been too thin and gangly, wore thick glasses and pulled her hair back in a drab ponytail for convenience. But she had bought a new dress for her first dinner with Jordan. He'd been polite and charming, and she'd returned home more in love than ever.

There was a second date. Hannah had found a reservoir of self-confidence in the wine, and when Jordan had suggested they stop at his apartment to pick up some papers before dropping her at her place, she'd agreed.

He gave her a tour of the apartment, and at the bedroom she found herself looping her arms around his neck and smiling up at him. Jordan took it from there. If there was a seduction, she had been a more than willing participant, if not the instigator. But that didn't assuage her anger with Jordan.

He was handsome, he was articulate, he was intelligent, he was the walking embodiment of charm. And he'd never called her again after they'd made love.

Her grandmother was right, she decided. Men only wanted one thing. And when they got it, they moved on to the next conquest.

Her pride stung, even more so when she'd passed Jordan's office two days later and had seen him in conference with a buxom blonde. Some conference. Her bosom was thrust into his face as she leaned over the desk next to him, and one hand with its manicured, fire-engine red press-on nails was draped teasingly over his.

Hannah would have continued working at McClennon Industries, would have continued with her dateless, colorless existence, because she was a Brewster, and that was what she had been taught. But circumstances intervened.

Her sister, Marybeth, the wild one in the family, had become pregnant out of wedlock, and Hannah had quit her job to help her out. When Hannah finally returned to St. Louis, it was with her sister's child and to a different job.

Until this day she had not seen Jordan McClennon again.

She nearly groaned at the sight of him. She might not be in love any longer, but her libido hadn't forgotten him.

He had the same chiseled features and black hair as his brothers. His eyes were blue, so light and yet intense, like the center of a flame.

And he was looking right at her. With interest.

Immediately her surprise turned to irritation. He hadn't changed. He was always on the lookout for a conquest. Obviously he didn't recognize her yet, or he would know that he'd made this particular conquest seven years ago.

Hannah kept her expression carefully neutral as a chattering Ronnie led the men toward her. To her dismay, she found that she couldn't quite make herself look away from Jordan.

Her pride, like an irate security guard, willed her eyes to move along and stop dawdling where they didn't belong. But her eyes were focused only on doing an inventory of Jordan McClennon's features.

His black hair, thick and gleaming like ebony in the sun, was flawless, just unruly enough to move in the breeze and yet provide the perfect frame for his striking face. No flaws in his bone structure, either; the hard, square chin and high cheekbones would have done a Viking proud. Eyes so light blue that they seemed preternatural were still fixed unwaveringly on her. The straight, aristocratic nose, the full, firm mouth that quirked up on one side in an assured, sardonic half smile....

Stop! she ordered herself. But still, her shameless eyes took in his hard, lean chest and thighs and the tight jeans that made all kinds of promises.

There was still no wedding ring on his finger.

Her face was growing warm.

She made herself smile as Ronnie introduced the brothers to her.

"Hannah Brewster?" Jordan repeated as if Ronnie's introduction had come as a complete surprise. "The Hannah Brewster who used to work at my company?"

Hannah felt a prick of irritation that he chose that particular description—employee—instead of something more familiar. Still, she forced herself to nod coolly.

Jordan surveyed her with obvious interest.

"You cut your hair. And got rid of the glasses."

Her irritation grew. He was looking at her as if she were a new chair he was considering buying for his patio.

"Actually, I kind of liked the glasses," he said, smiling.

Hannah was determined not to let that charming smile do her in this time.

"I gave the glasses to charity when I got contacts," she

said dryly. "I didn't keep the hair, either, or you'd be welcome to it."

Jordan laughed, and she felt a pang, remembering how much she had liked his laugh once upon a time. It was like the sound of a river rolling over sun-warmed stones. It was the kind of laugh a woman liked to hear on a Saturday night while the radio played love songs and her lover slowly undressed her. It was a laugh—and a voice—that could warm the coldest night.

His eyes were studying her again. "No," he said softly. "I take it back about the glasses. Your eyes are too pretty to hide behind glasses."

From the corners of those eyes she could see his brothers exchanging glances. Apparently they were all too familiar with his routine.

"You must have a subscription to the *Guide for the Single Male*," she said sharply. "That's about the tenth time I've heard that line." She was making no concessions to his studied charm.

Jordan's smile widened, and she noticed that his brothers had raised their eyebrows in surprise.

"Pardon me, ma'am," the brother introduced as Jake said. "But could I take a picture of this? The great Jordan McClennon striking out with a woman?"

He and his other brother, John, laughed and punched a put-upon Jordan in the shoulder, grinning at Hannah as they turned to leave.

"It was nice meeting you, Hannah," John, the middle McClennon brother, said. "*Very* nice. Come on, Ronnie. Let's get to work."

Hannah scrambled to her feet, picked up the board and cradled it in her arms. When she felt Jordan encroaching too closely on her heels, she turned suddenly, nearly catching him in the stomach with the board's end.

"Hannah, I—" he began, the laughter gone from his face.

"Excuse me, Jordan," she interrupted crisply. "I'm here

to help Ronnie build a house, and that's all. Don't waste your energy on me.'' With that, she turned with as much dignity as she could muster, the board still in her arms like a soldier's musket, and trooped toward the cement foundation.

Hannah leaned on the board and carefully avoided looking at Jordan as she watched Jake gather tools from the back of the pickup. A long strip of metal lay half-coiled on the ground by her feet. Glancing down, she caught a distorted reflection of herself, and studied it impassively.

She supposed she did look quite different from the way Jordan had remembered. Her short haircut with its pixie bangs and tousled shape gave her fine brown hair more character and suited her face. She used mascara now that her brown eyes were actually visible without glasses, and it had seemed a natural progression to wear a light shade of lipstick as well.

She had always tended to be on the thin side, but over the past few years she had gained enough weight to add some curves. She was wearing an old pair of jeans that clung to her rounded hips, and a pink cotton T-shirt with a picture of a hot-fudge sundae on the front above the words Breakfast Of Champions. She was all too aware that the T-shirt stretched tightly over her breasts.

Thinking back, she had never known what it was that prompted Jordan McClennon to ask her out in the first place. At the time it had seemed a miracle that someone like Jordan would notice mousy little Hannah Brewster, much less take her to dinner.

Her affair with Jordan had been the only one in her life, and it had taught her a valuable lesson about herself. She was not the promiscuous type, and she was not about to let anything like that happen again. Her sister, rest her soul, had occupied enough beds to fill a motel directory, but that life-style was not for Hannah. She would rather remain celibate than repeat the humiliation of making love with a man she cared for, only to have him waltz away with not so much as a backward glance.

Jake returned with a power saw and hammers and began explaining the framing of a house, as John helped him set up the saw. Hannah began to get cold feet about the whole project as Jake talked about how they were going to build the sill.

She didn't belong here at all, she assured herself. She had some skill with a hammer and saw only because she had helped her father—if helped was the right word—when he remodeled their house. She had done it because she'd wanted to be with him, and she had treasured those times together. But she was here now simply because she was Ronnie's friend. And he was the only reason she hadn't headed back to St. Louis already.

Ronnie had been an electronically precocious but socially oblivious teenager when he'd begun working at McClennon Industries as a summer intern. Hannah had been a few years older, but she had befriended him when she'd seen him eating his lunch alone, a stoic look on his face. She'd lost touch with him when she left McClennon Industries, but when she returned to St. Louis, she ran into him again at the library where she worked. She had visited him in Sandford a couple of times, and she was fond of his mother, Esther.

Jake and John were laying the metal strip over the foundation rim now, and Jake called to Jordan to get the sill boards ready. Hannah met Jordan's eyes briefly before he moved toward the tarp-covered pile of lumber. She felt her pulse quicken.

"I'm sorry," Ronnie said lamely beside her. "I didn't know that Jake had told Jordan about the house. I didn't have any idea he'd be here."

Hannah ended Ronnie's misery with a gentle touch on his arm. "It's okay. There's no reason to feel awkward. It's been a long time since I last saw Jordan, and, believe me, there's no spark there anymore."

The last part wasn't entirely true, but Ronnie seemed satisfied.

He moved off to help Jake and John, and Hannah studied Jordan covertly. How had she forgotten how physically compelling he was? Maybe it was a case of not wanting to remember. It all seemed like a dream now. That she had once been intimate with this man made the blood collect in places that hadn't felt a man's touch since Jordan.

What he had done to her, she thought in wonder, was to seduce her with the expertise of long practice. No, that wasn't quite fair. She'd been more than willing to be seduced. And it had been an exquisite experience.

But a man like Jordan McClennon knew how good he was with women. And Hannah realized with certainty that he would seduce her all over again if he could. For him it would be just another game.

"Hannah!" Jordan called sharply, startling her and making her blush as if he had read her thoughts. "Help me with these boards."

She was tempted to tell him to do it himself, but she realized that both Jake and John were watching, though they tried not to be obvious about it. She decided it was less trying to help with the boards than to be the continuing source of the McClennon brothers' amusement.

"Well?" she said, frowning, as Jordan continued to watch her, his eyes narrowed.

"You're standing on the board, Hannah," he explained with exaggerated patience. "That makes it a little tough for me to pick it up. Not that you're not light as a feather, sweetheart, but I haven't had my Wheaties today."

"You mean there's something you can't do?" she shot back. She had never been particularly defensive before now, but this was the man who had seen her naked, who had made love to her, then left her.

His eyes met hers and held. "Shall I come over there and move you?" he asked quietly.

His voice was too low for anyone else to hear, but the

heat climbed her face, anyway. The arrogant egotist would probably love an excuse to touch her. No doubt he thought she would fall all over him again.

Lifting her chin, Hannah stepped to the side, then bent and grasped the end of the board. With one last look at her, Jordan did the same.

"Is it too heavy?" he asked solicitously, and she grunted negatively, determined not to give him any more response than absolutely necessary.

When they had deposited the last of the boards on the ground by the foundation, Hannah put her hands on her lower back and stretched. She wasn't badly out of shape, but it had been a long time since Kevin had been light enough for her to lift him with any frequency. That was the trouble with babies; they eventually grew up. It seemed that every day they presented their mothers with a new set of problems and a new set of delights. She gently touched the locket at her neck. It still saddened Hannah that Marybeth never got to see her son turn into such a wonderful kid.

"Are you all right?" Jordan asked carefully, and Hannah focused on him, realizing that she had been staring off into the distance.

"Yes," she said with resignation. She had learned how to be all right no matter what happened. She supposed she had inherited from her father the ability to put one foot in front of the other and soldier on despite any difficulty. Not that it was always easy; there were more than enough times when she nearly wondered aloud why she was bothering. But a Brewster didn't stop to ask pointless questions when there was work to be done.

Jake had finished attaching the metal strip to the foundation and was moving the first sill board into place. Ronnie appeared by Hannah's side and with an encouraging smile handed her a hammer. Jordan didn't miss the fact that Ronnie's fingers brushed Hannah's. Turning her back on Jordan, Hannah bent to pick up some nails.

Jordan studied her while his brothers drilled holes for the anchor bolts. He vaguely remembered the restaurant where he'd taken her to dinner a long time ago. What he remembered vividly was the sensation of her, of Hannah Brewster. There was a vitality in her, a warmth that made a man feel good all over just looking at her or listening to her talk.

He marveled that he could remember that evening so clearly. He had tugged her toward his bedroom when they had reached his apartment, and she had gone willingly. He could still see the smile on her face as she put her arms around his neck. He had taken her glasses off for her and then unfastened her hair, letting it fan out across the pillow. She had been nervous, fumbling with his buttons until he had to undo his shirt himself. But she had been so sweet in his bed.

He still hadn't quite figured out the parameters of her relationship with Ronnie, but maybe it was one of those steadfast, quiet love affairs devoid of overt displays of affection. He couldn't imagine why else she would be here— carpentry skills or not—unless there was something between her and the red-haired electronics prodigy.

Jordan realized that he was thinking, at least on a subconscious level, of taking her to bed again. She had grown into a beautiful woman since he had last seen her. Not that she hadn't been attractive before—she just hadn't known it then. She had a quiet confidence about her now. Still, something was missing.

Her smile—that was it. It was what had first drawn him to her. And he had yet to see it today.

He supposed she smiled for Ronnie. Resolutely he sat down on the ground by the pile of tools, rummaging for another hammer. He told himself to stop thinking about Hannah Brewster. She was treating him with all the welcome of a spitting cat. It was plain that she didn't want anything to do with him.

Which made her all the more intriguing.

"I need the nails," she said stoically, and he glanced up to see her silhouetted in the sun, her hands on her hips.

"What nails?" he asked stupidly, so lost in thinking about her that he was unsure for a moment if he was looking at her or a memory.

"The nine-gauge," she said in the calm, efficient tone she'd apparently adopted just for him. "You're sitting on them," she added pointedly.

Jordan frowned, looking around the grass where he was sitting. "I think I'd know if I was sitting on nails," he assured her.

"Maybe your jeans have cut off the circulation to your brain," she suggested with a slight curve of her mouth, letting him know just where she thought he kept his brain.

"Hannah," he began impatiently, wondering just what it was he wanted to say to her now that he'd started.

"Ah!" she said suddenly, diving down and scooping up a paper bag. "See, I told you," she said, straightening with the bag of nails.

She was giving him back as good as he'd given her when she had been standing on the board, and it took him by surprise. Few women argued with him, much less provoked him.

"I *wasn't* sitting on them," he insisted. He shifted his weight forward, intent on standing so he could have this argument face-to-face, when his thigh came down on something sharp. "Ow," he muttered, reaching down and closing his hand around metal. He held up a hasp. "*That's* what I was sitting on," he said.

For a moment she almost smiled, but in the next instant the smile was gone before it really materialized, leaving him bereft. He wondered why it mattered so much to him that she wouldn't smile for him. And why it aggravated him so.

* * *

Hannah knew she was getting on his nerves. She could see it in his puzzled frown and in the set of his mouth. She found that she rather liked getting on his nerves. It was something that she would never have thought to do seven years ago.

"Carpenters!" Jake called out. "We need some carpenters with hammers over here!"

Hannah and Jordan both turned at once, Hannah scrambling toward Jake and John, unable to stop herself from watching from the corner of her eye as Jordan hefted a hammer before he followed. How old was he now? she wondered. Thirty-two. In his prime. A walking, talking, thirty-two-year-old specimen of temptation. She was only three years younger, but she often had the feeling that she had missed out on some part of her twenties that was important. She didn't know how to flirt, and she didn't know how to tell men things they wanted to hear.

Jordan knelt beside her, swiftly hammering in a nail at the joint next to the one she had just finished. His thigh was so close to her that the denim lightly brushed her hip, making her fingers shake as she searched in the bag for another nail. Unwillingly she remembered how that thigh had felt naked, hard and muscular along the length of her own leg. She stared down at the board in front of her.

She could feel him watching her, and she was sure he knew what effect he was having on her. She was almost positive that he was provoking this physical contact deliberately to pay her back for her cool treatment of him. Either that or he was intent on luring her into his bed again—and that was never going to happen.

He reached across her for another nail, and his firm hand brushed her bare arm, the contact, brief as it was, igniting heat that flared across her skin. She was trembling inside, hoping it didn't show. She wouldn't let him see how addled he was making her. Her flash point reaction to his casual touch could be easily explained by her long celibacy, she rationalized.

"So, what accounts for your expertise?" he asked suddenly, throwing her off guard.

"What?" She forgot about her rehearsed indifference and looked into his eyes. A mistake. They were far too probing, and she hastily looked away.

"The hammering," he said. "Where did you learn carpentry?"

"From my father," she said shortly. "I helped when he remodeled our house about twelve years ago. He taught me a lot. Sometimes I helped him when he accepted outside carpentry work."

"Did we talk about that when we went out?" he asked, surprised.

This time she looked at him deliberately, meeting his eyes and making sure he saw her coolness.

"Frankly, Jordan, I doubt that you'd remember much of anything I told you then," she said. "I don't think conversation was your prime objective." She wanted to make sure he understood that she hadn't mistaken their prior involvement for anything more than it was—an office affair, short and meaningless.

It had been so much more to her. She could remember almost every word of their conversations, even if Jordan couldn't.

Abruptly she stood and moved to another corner of the foundation, deftly hammering in two nails where the sill boards joined.

Jordan followed her, squatting beside her, far too close for her comfort.

"That house your father remodeled," he said. "Does he still live there?"

"He died a few years ago," she said flatly, reaching for another nail even though two were sufficient.

"I'm sorry," he said.

"Are you?" she asked sharply, looking into his face. "Or is it just the polite thing to say?" She was aware that she'd spoken a little too loudly, and now Ronnie and Jordan's brothers were staring at her, the sounds of hammers and drills having ceased for the moment.

"I don't know what's wrong here," Jordan said carefully. "What have I done, Hannah?"

"Nothing," she said, lying, but still managing to sound tired and aggrieved, something she hated when other women did it. If something was wrong, a person should just come out and say it. At least that was what she believed. But this wasn't the time or the place to get specific, not when half of Jordan's family was listening with intense interest.

"Hey!" a commanding woman's voice called over the whine of a car engine. "Who wants something to eat?"

Hannah turned as a battered, fluorescent orange Volkswagen churned the driveway's gravel amid the grinding of gears. The car overshot the end of the driveway by a good five feet, coming to rest just inches from a scarred oak tree that looked like it had had more than its share of close encounters with the VW if the flecks of orange paint on the bark were any indication. Ronnie's sigh was audible.

"Hi, Ma. How come you're here so early?"

"Early, schmearly. I figured you wouldn't think to feed these folks. Now was I right or was I right?"

"Yeah, Ma, you're right," Ronnie agreed, shifting his weight from one foot to the other.

The portly woman in the green waitress uniform arched an eyebrow at him as she passed, trailing the scent of hamburgers in her wake. She smiled at Hannah as she set a large white bag on the foundation.

"Now, Hannah, these boys haven't been working you too hard, have they?" she asked.

"Not even hard enough to earn a meal, Esther," Hannah said, smiling despite her recent bitter exchange with Jordan.

Esther turned toward the car. "Kevin, if you want a hamburger, you'd better get over here." She winked at Hannah. "He's been busing and setting up tables for me all morning."

"He hasn't gotten in your way, has he?" Hannah asked. "I could watch him here."

"The time a little boy gets in my way, honey," Esther told her, "is the day that Esther Wardlow retires. He's been an angel. Best bus boy we ever had," she added in a loud voice as Kevin hopped from the car and trooped over to her, grinning at his mother.

"Look, Mom!" he called excitedly, holding out one small hand with four quarters on his palm. "I got tips. See? I'm rich. I done good, huh?"

Hannah couldn't help smiling and gave him a short hug. He was such a good boy, always cheerful, always excited about something. He had her brown hair and eyes, but her sister's short nose and bow-shaped mouth.

"Very good," she said, tousling his hair. "I might even let you spend your fortune on some bubble gum since you worked so hard."

"Really?"

"Really. I'm feeling generous. Are you hungry?"

Kevin shook his head. "I ate pancakes for breakfast and some toast and some bacon and some—" he wrinkled his nose, trying to think "—some sausages," he concluded with satisfaction.

And this was the child who claimed he was never hungry in the morning, she thought, giving a mental sigh.

"I think you're going to have to bus some more tables to pay for all that food," she informed him. "Someday you'll eat me out of house and home."

Kevin laughed and danced up and down, clearly delighted with his mother's familiar but good-natured complaint.

The men had gathered around the bag to get a hamburger, and Hannah glanced up to find Jordan still squatting by the foundation, his pensive eyes on her.

Good, she thought. Let him catch sight of a kid, and Mr. I'm-So-Irresistible will turn tail and run. And leave me alone.

"All right, sport," Esther said to Kevin. "Let's get going before the lunch crowd pours in."

"I got work to do," Kevin informed the group importantly, jabbing his thumb toward his chest and walking cockily to the car.

"Make sure you do a good job," Hannah called after him. "Remember what I told you."

"A Brewster always does his best," he parroted as if he'd said the words a hundred times. But he smiled at her and waved as Esther backed the car erratically out of the driveway.

Hannah could feel Jordan watching her, but she carefully plucked a hamburger from the bag and sat on the ground a cautious distance away. She found it hard to eat when Jordan sat down right next to her. The other three men settled a few feet away, obviously interested in whatever was going on between Jordan and Hannah.

So, Jordan thought, Ronnie wasn't sitting next to her. Maybe he'd misunderstood the situation.

"Nice kid," Jordan said, clearing his throat.

It hadn't escaped him that Kevin's last name was apparently Brewster. So Hannah hadn't married the kid's father.

"They don't come any better," she agreed, her eyes on her food, her knees bent and pulled defensively to her chest. "I'd walk through fire for that child."

He knew that she meant it. And he knew that somewhere in her words there was a warning aimed at him. He just didn't know what to make of it.

Hannah was obviously self-sufficient and strong, far more sure of herself now than she'd been when he first knew her.

"So," he said, swallowing a bite and leaning back against the pile of lumber, "do you come up here to Sandford often?"

Hannah turned to look at him, frowning. If this was another of his pick-up lines, it wasn't going to work.

"I've been here a few times," she offered, going back

to her hamburger. "Ronnie asked me to plan a birthday party for his mother last winter. And Esther, the incurable matchmaker, has invited me here several times on one pretext or another to meet the latest eligible bachelor truck driver who stops at the diner."

"She keeps fixing you up, huh?" Jordan asked, perking up.

"She tries, bless her," Hannah said. "If she's not working on me, she's digging up girls for Ronnie."

A very satisfied smile crossed Jordan's face.

Hannah couldn't seem to avoid Jordan the rest of the day, not when he followed her and worked right next to her during the entire framing process. But she did manage to keep her mind off him by dint of the hard physical labor that went into building a house.

By nightfall her back ached and her hands burned, but her mind was too peacefully exhausted to dwell on the dark-haired man who had shadowed her steps all day.

It was late when Esther fed them all spaghetti and insisted on cleaning up the dishes herself. Hannah heard the McClennons and Ronnie leave, the low hum of the truck motors fading into the twilight.

Hannah took Kevin to the spare bedroom in Esther's trailer and read to him from one of his favorite books, the story of two misbehaving insects. Then she tucked Kevin in bed and kissed his forehead as he smiled sleepily.

"Close your eyes," she said, beginning the ritual that ended each night for mother and son.

"Sweet sleep," he responded.

"Dream a dream…"

"For me to keep."

He was tired from the excitement of helping Esther all day in the restaurant, and she smiled as she watched his breathing soften almost as soon as his eyes closed.

Dream a dream for me to keep, she repeated in her head as she stepped into the dark hallway. Kevin was her dream now, though he had been thrust upon her before she had time to realize what was happening.

Marybeth, she whispered under her breath, *you don't know how much I love him.*

Hannah had helped her sister financially and emotionally all through her pregnancy, but Marybeth had never been interested in motherhood. She'd been enamored of rock musicians and lived the uncertain, hazardous life of a groupie. The boy who fathered Kevin—though determining exactly which boy was impossible—had no interest in parenthood, either.

Hannah had taken in the baby each time Marybeth went off on one of her road trips with her latest heavy metal band of the hour. Hannah knew that Marybeth was no saint on those trips, and she had strongly resisted hearing any of the details. But, nevertheless, it was a shock the day a young policeman came to her door to tell her that her only living relative had died of a drug overdose in a motel room three hundred miles away.

Hannah had gone to court to gain formal custody of Kevin, and it was granted. She had inherited her parents' house when they died, and she had let Marybeth live there rent free. After her sister was gone, Hannah had sold the house and invested the proceeds in a mutual fund, using the dividends to help defray the costs of raising a child.

She was frugal, and when she returned to St. Louis she got a job at a branch library that paid enough to provide a reasonable life-style for a young mother and child.

Day care was trickier, but she had managed through careful budgeting to put Kevin in a cheerful, responsible center when he was younger. And once he started school she arranged her work schedule so that she could get home most days before he did. When she had to work weekends or the evening shift, she paid a mature, neighborhood teen to baby-sit.

She had planned carefully, and she had worked to give Kevin a good life. The only thing she hadn't been prepared for was the fierce love she felt for the boy she considered her son. She had never known an emotion like it, and she found it humbling.

She reached up now to touch the locket with the picture of her and Marybeth and Kevin when he was a baby. Her fingers fumbled when they didn't find it. Hannah went into the bathroom, turned on the light and searched the mirror, even shook out her T-shirt. But it was gone.

"Oh, *damn*," she whispered under her breath. She must have lost it while she was working outside. It could be anywhere in the grass.

She knew she should just go to bed and worry about it in the morning, but the locket was important to her. It was virtually all she had left of her sister, all Kevin had left. It was the only photograph she had found when she'd sold the house.

A single lamp burned in the living room, and Hannah surmised from the flickering bluish light under the door of the main bedroom that Esther had retired to watch the old movies that were her addiction.

Hannah had insisted she could sleep on the convertible couch, and Esther had reluctantly given in.

Hannah went about quietly rummaging for a flashlight, finally coming across one under the sink. Slipping out the door, she closed it softly behind her and switched on the flashlight. It flickered errantly but steadied when she shook it. Good, she thought. It was especially bright, just what she needed.

She could smell the herbs that Esther had planted near the door as she stepped off the concrete block onto the ground. She stood quietly a moment, letting her eyes adjust to the dark. She walked a few more steps into the yard, pausing to look up at the sky. The stars seemed unnaturally bright to her after years of living in the city where street-lights muted the sky.

But she wasn't here to stargaze. The most likely place for her locket was around the foundation where she'd been hammering most of the day. In the starlight she could see the section of house frame in place over the subflooring, like a skeleton against the sky. It gave her a strong sense of satisfaction to know she had helped put it there.

She was on her knees a moment later, crawling along the foundation, feeling in the grass with her hands while she shone the light on the ground.

"It's a bit dark to hunt mushrooms, you know."

She was so startled that she jumped, banging her head against one of the cross braces.

"Ow!" she cried out, losing her balance and ending up sitting on the grass, her back against the foundation. She rubbed her head where it hurt and glared up at Jordan, who looked like a giant silhouetted against the starry sky.

"Are you all right?" he asked, kneeling in front of her. He put his hand on her shoulder as if to check.

"I'm…fine," she managed to snap. "What are you doing out here?"

"That's what I was asking you," he said.

"You didn't ask," she corrected him indignantly. "You just made some nitwit remark about mushrooms."

"Nitwit," Jordan muttered under his breath, and even in the dark she could see his frown. "Speaking of nitwits, *I'm* not the one skulking around in the middle of the night."

"And just what would you call what you're doing?" she demanded.

"I was sleeping—at least until you started shining that damn beacon all over the place."

"Sleeping?" she repeated in disbelief. "Where?"

"In my camper," he said irritably, and she squinted at the driveway, barely able to make out the shape of his truck.

Hannah realized she was still clutching the flashlight in her right hand, and she pointed it at Jordan's face, still confused as to why he was here.

"Will you cut that out?" he complained. "You're going

to blind me in a minute." The hand on her shoulder had tightened, infuriating her all the more.

"*You're* the one who scared me half to death," she said, pointedly aiming the light at his face again. "What were you doing creeping up on me if you were sleeping?"

"I told you," he said, his voice rising. "The light woke me up. You were shining it around the yard like some halogen come-on at a car lot."

"'Come-on!'" She was truly furious now, and she moved to get to her feet, succeeding in nearly blinding him with the light once more. "You certainly have a big ego if you think I'm coming on to you, buster!" she informed him, waving the light about in her agitation.

Jordan took hold of the flashlight, but Hannah held on obstinately.

"I didn't say you were coming on to me," he argued.

"Well, I certainly was not," she insisted.

"Hannah!" he said between clenched teeth. "Will you kindly let go of the flashlight!"

But she wasn't about to do anything he wanted, kindly or otherwise. She jerked back on the flashlight and felt her sneakers slip on the wet grass.

The next thing she knew she was on her back with Jordan hovering over her. One of his hands was braced beside her head while the other held the flashlight. She was still so angry with him that she pushed against his chest to put some distance between them. Instantly she was aware of the hardness and warmth beneath her hands, and she froze.

The expression on Jordan's face changed, as well. He had been irritated with her before, she knew, but now there was something akin to confusion sweeping his features.

He stared at her a long moment in the dark, his hand curled around the flashlight so tightly that his knuckles stood out in stark relief. His face was only inches from hers. An old memory came rushing back of this same face so close to hers as he made love to her. He was the man who had tutored her in the art of lovemaking, and even though it had been one time only, she had never forgotten it.

Hannah had to bite back a groan as her fingers lessened their pressure to fan out over his chest. She couldn't look away from his face. He was even more mesmerizing now than he'd been seven years ago.

Slowly his mouth lowered to hers as if he wanted to stop himself but couldn't. Hannah felt her breath release on a sigh as his lips finally touched hers. Her hands curled around the fabric of his shirt.

She could feel him start to draw away, but then he gave in to the need that they both felt and deepened the kiss. Hannah responded, her hands moving to the back of his neck, touching his hair and letting her fingers luxuriate in the silkiness of it. She was kissing him back with all the need of a woman who had not felt the touch of a man for too long.

When Jordan raised his head, she saw something new in his eyes, something that made her wary.

"I've been wanting to do that all day," he told her, his breathing not quite slowed to normal. "And there are a million other things I've been wanting to do, too."

The blood rushed to her face as the full impact of what she'd just done hit her. He had been toying with her, luring her into his bed again, and he was sure he had made her compliant. She was so mortified that she abruptly dropped her hands from his neck and tried to stand up.

But he was ahead of her, standing and pulling her to her feet by her shoulders. She felt a rush of cool air across the dew-dampened back of her clothes.

"You can forget about those other things you're wanting to do," she said, trying to will her voice to coolness when she still felt out of breath. "I'm not interested."

"No?" he said, investing the word with both skepticism and amusement. He caught her arm, pulling her to him, and for one breathless moment she thought he was going to kiss her again. But he made no move toward her. "There's no sin in wanting someone, Hannah. And we're hardly strangers.''

"We're strangers as far as I'm concerned," she told him, standing stiffly in his grip. "I made a mistake a long time ago, and I don't intend to repeat it."

He abruptly let her go, and Hannah turned, hugging her arms to herself as she hurried toward the trailer. She thought he said something softly, something she couldn't quite make out, but she went on without missing a step. It sounded like "We'll see."

Once inside, she ran a weary hand through her hair. She had left the flashlight with him, and she hadn't looked for her locket, but right now she was glad just to have escaped without humiliating herself any more than she had. She stood at the side of the window, looking out into the dark and letting her heartbeat slow to normal.

He was far too attractive and far too sure of himself. And she was...

Just what was she? she wondered. *Lonely.* Despite her son and her job, she was lonely, and that made her all too vulnerable.

"I thought I heard something," Esther said from behind her, and Hannah jumped, spinning around.

"Your back is wet," Esther said with concern. The next instant they both heard the truck tailgate slam with unnecessary force.

Hannah felt her face turn red. She knew her hair was disheveled, as well, and she didn't have a ready explanation.

"Jordan and I were talking," she said awkwardly.

"Honey," Esther said with a significant glance at the window, "you was doing more than talking unless that man spit all over your back. And that's all I got to say on the matter." She turned and went back to her bedroom, her floral nightgown billowing in her wake.

Hannah stifled a groan of frustration. She knew she wasn't going to sleep well that night.

Two

Hannah awoke to the sound of nearby giggling and the smell of bacon frying. The curtains were drawn, leaving her disoriented in the dim light. The giggling came again, and she recognized Kevin's voice.

She must have overslept. She sat up in consternation, searching with her feet for her slippers. Something was going on behind her, but the couch where she'd slept was right up against the partition that separated it from the kitchen, so all she was getting through the wall were those giggles and muffled talking.

She glanced at her portable alarm clock and saw that it was seven. Apparently, she hadn't heard Esther leave for work.

Hannah shuffled around the partition, stopping short when she saw that Jordan was there with Kevin. And Jordan was *cooking?*

Her disbelief must have registered on her face, because Jordan laughed when he saw her and motioned her to come closer. She didn't miss the fact that his eyes traveled down her length appreciatively before he carefully looked at her face. "We're working on masterpieces," he informed her.

"Come here and see!" Kevin called, impatiently waving his arm to get her to come to the stove.

Still bemused by the sight of Jordan in a domestic setting, Hannah went to the stove and peered over Kevin's head. They were cooking pancakes. Or doing something indefinable with pancakes, she decided. Four of them sat on the griddle, two with strange marks on them, which, on closer inspection, she realized were faces. Kevin was in the process of drawing on the third with a small paintbrush and...chocolate syrup?

Hannah looked at the open can of chocolate syrup on the counter and then back at the pancakes. "What are you doing?" she asked, totally at a loss.

"Making faces," Kevin informed her as if she were the densest mother in the world. "See?"

"I see. I just don't believe." She glanced at Jordan, finding him watching her with an expression she could only describe as interested.

"Do you have any idea what Esther used those brushes for?" she demanded of Jordan.

He shrugged, his eyes full of mischief. "Oh, I'm sure she doesn't need them. They were just lying under the sink in an old can with—" He broke off and laughed at her horrified expression. "Actually, they were brand new, still in their wrappers," he told her.

"But...chocolate," she said, knowing that she should be aghast at something, but just not quite sure what it was.

"You were extolling the virtues of chocolate on your shirt yesterday," he reminded her. "Don't you ever do something just because it's fun?" he demanded suddenly.

"I can't afford fun," she told him with absolute honesty.

"Are you financially or emotionally bankrupt?" he asked quietly, turning back to the stove to lift the pancakes onto a plate.

She would have taken offense at his question, but she knew that he was right. She was very close to being emotionally bankrupt. And he was partially to blame for that.

"Don't you think you should let me clean this up a little?" she suggested, eyeing the kitchen counter awash in their used cooking utensils and spilled ingredients.

"Don't you think you should put on a robe?" he countered, his eyes taking in her length again, this time lingering on her breasts.

Belatedly she realized she was standing near a window, her body all too visible through the thin cotton fabric of her nightgown. Flushing, she turned and left the room.

From the other side of the partition, she heard her son say, "Mom's not a morning person."

Just great, she thought. As if succumbing to Jordan McClennon's charms wasn't enough, now she had a family member making excuses for her behavior.

Hannah gathered up clean clothes from the small suitcase she'd left on the floor and carried them to the bathroom.

She definitely looked like a woman who'd had a near sleepless night because of the man in Esther's kitchen. Hannah sighed. It wouldn't do to look this tired when Ronnie and Jordan's brothers arrived. They seemed all too adept at sizing up the situation. And far too interested in what was going on between her and Jordan.

She still couldn't believe she'd actually seen him painting chocolate faces on pancakes. "No end to his talents," she muttered to herself, but that made her blush again as she thought of his lusty lovemaking so long ago. And no doubt he'd had the opportunity to practice it many times since, on one besotted female after another.

She came into the kitchen dressed in her jeans and a clean T-shirt, this one a plain black.

"No message this time, I see," Jordan said, looking up from the table where he was eating and grinning at her T-shirt's simplicity.

"I don't want to be the instigator of any more dietary

disasters," she said. But she nearly smiled back at him. It was almost impossible not to be taken in by him.

Until she realized what it was that her son was crunching.

"Potato chips?" she said in disbelief. "You're eating potato chips for breakfast?"

"Esther doesn't have any hash browns, Mom," Kevin explained earnestly.

A strong lecture on fat and sodium was in order, but glancing at Jordan's sheepish face sapped her determination. She had lost control long before she got out of bed, and she might as well acknowledge that fact.

"Here," Jordan said, standing and holding a chair for her. "I'll get you some breakfast."

"No chocolate pancakes or potato chips, please," she said, sighing.

"Bacon sandwich then," he said, popping two slices of bread into the toaster and slipping the leftover bacon into the microwave. "And coffee."

She really wasn't a morning person, he thought, smiling to himself as he listened to her talk to Kevin about the importance of him staying out of the way today. "We brought your books, and the TV's right here," she told him.

"Can't I hammer just one nail?" he begged.

Hannah shook her head. "I don't want you to hit someone's thumb instead," she said, reaching out to tousle his hair. "Especially mine." She made a face at him, and Kevin laughed.

Kevin reminded Jordan of Jake's daughter, Molly. Molly was a little older. He didn't remember anyone saying how old Kevin was, but the boy had told him something this morning about a picnic coming up soon to celebrate the end of first grade. That was a big milestone in a kid's life.

He carried a cup of coffee to the table for Hannah, distracted from his thoughts when she smiled at him. How he liked her smile! He could imagine a man doing all sorts of things just to earn one. He glanced at Kevin again and wondered why the boy's father hadn't stayed around for those smiles.

But he had no time to dwell on that. He heard the truck pulling up outside and started carrying dishes to the sink. He would have plenty of time to ponder the intricacies of Hannah Brewster's life while he pounded nails today.

They had worked on the frame most of the morning, stopping only when Esther showed up again with hamburgers shortly before noon. Hannah had kept one eye on the grass while she worked, looking for her locket, but to no avail. Now they sat on the ground, resting their backs against the pile of lumber, and ate. Esther sat on the cement block that served as a step at her trailer door, her knees spread wide, her uniform skirt sagging between her legs. She was lecturing Ronnie on his lack of a love life despite her best efforts, and he was turning scarlet from his ears to the patch of pale chest that showed above his V-neck shirt. Kevin was listening with avid interest.

Jordan grinned, amused by the whole idea of Esther orchestrating a romance.

"It's time you thought about settling down," Esther told him. "And Lord knows I've broken my neck checking out possibilities for you. Don't you grin at me, Jake McClennon," she said ominously, catching him before he ducked his head to his burger. "I got you married now, didn't I?"

"Yes, Esther," Jake said dutifully, still trying to hide his grin. "Though I can't quite recall exactly how you got Laura and me together."

Esther harrumphed. "Of course not. I ain't obvious when it comes to affairs of the heart, so to speak. I took your problem to St. Jude, and he took care of the details."

"St. Jude?" Hannah asked, realizing she'd opened a whole new can of worms when the men around her groaned.

"The patron saint of hopeless causes," Esther informed

her, shooting a dark look at each man in turn. "And, believe me, those McClennon boys were certainly hopeless causes when it came to marriage." She brushed crumbs from her skirt like a duchess smoothing a fine swath of silk. "But I got my St. Jude statue, and he's done come through for me many a time."

"It's more like a concrete elf she keeps behind the diner," Jordan informed her in a low voice.

"I heard that!" Esther snorted. "And I don't care what he looks like, he's *my* St. Jude and he knows me!" Her eyes took in each member of the group, stopping on Jordan.

"I surrender," Jordan said immediately, throwing his hands into the air as his brothers and Ronnie laughed. "When is St. Jude's next miracle?"

Esther narrowed her eyes, looking from Jordan to Hannah until Hannah felt the heat climbing her neck.

"Maybe sooner than you think," Esther said with satisfaction. "Could be you're the next one on his list, Jordan. Might want to start pricing fancy suits for your wedding."

"Not Jordan," John said with conviction. "The day he gets married is the day I'll dance naked around that St. Jude statue."

Over the laughter Jake said, "And I'll play the kazoo while he does it."

Esther raised her brows. "Then maybe you'd better go get yourself some lessons at the Arthur Murray Dance Studio," she told John tartly.

When the laughter subsided, they all slowly stretched their muscles and walked back toward the frame. Jordan picked up a hammer and listened idly as Kevin asked Esther more questions about St. Jude.

"Do you think he'd help me get something special for my birthday?" he was asking seriously. "I'm gonna be seven. It's not until October, but I figure a kid has to start planning early."

"Now I don't know," Esther said. "Depends on what it is you want."

"Well," Kevin said as he dug his toe into the ground, obviously reluctant to come right out with it. "Let's just say it's something every kid wants."

"Can't be more specific?" Esther prodded.

Kevin's voice dropped, and Jordan strained to hear. "It's got legs and a face and hair and all that stuff."

"Hmm," Esther said. "A pony?"

"No, no," Kevin said plaintively. "A dad. You know, someone I could do stuff with. He doesn't got to live with my mom. Lots of kids at school got dads who don't live with their moms. I'm not picky."

He sounded so earnest and wistful that Jordan felt a chord of sympathy for the boy. Why didn't Hannah have any contact with Kevin's father? At least then the kid would have a token dad.

"Well," Esther said, "we'll have to talk to St. Jude about this. I don't know if he'll be able to help or not, but we'll see."

"Can I go back to work with you now so we can talk to him right away?" Kevin asked eagerly.

"I don't see why not," Esther said. "Let's go tell your mother."

Jordan glanced over his shoulder and saw that Hannah was working too far away to have heard the exchange. Just as well, he thought. It would be one more thing for her to worry about.

Methodically he began driving nails into the cross brace in front of him.

So Kevin would be seven this October. That meant he was born in...

He mentally made the calculation while continuing to hammer. And Hannah would have conceived him nine months before that, in January of that year.

Jordan frowned. Something was there in the back of his memory. Something else that had happened in January of that year.

His loan. That was it. He'd received the loan that had

enabled him to expand the business that month. He'd gone out to celebrate with...

Hannah.

He'd taken her out to dinner, and they'd ended up back at his apartment, toasting the growth of McClennon Industries.

And then they had made love. *About nine months before Kevin Brewster was born.*

The hammer came down again, but he was in such a state of shock that he paid no attention to his aim.

Hannah nearly dropped her own hammer when she heard him howl in pain. John, Jake and Ronnie were already racing toward him, and Esther, about to get into her car with Kevin, bustled back toward the work site as well.

Hannah danced around on tiptoe, straining to see over the shoulders of the McClennon brothers, but they were too tall, and with all of her bobbing she was beginning to feel like a kernel of popcorn on a hot skillet.

"He'll live," Esther pronounced, and Jake and John clapped Jordan on the back.

"Getting a little clumsy in our old age, aren't we, brother?" John asked dryly.

"There was a bee," Jordan said, but his alibi sounded a little weak to Hannah. "It buzzed me, and I missed the nail."

"Hannah!" Esther called. "Take Jordan inside and put some cream on his thumb."

"Me?" Hannah said from the back of the group, trying to think of a way to avoid the assignment. "I don't know where it is."

"Above the kitchen sink in the left-hand cupboard," Esther said. "I'd do it myself, but I'm already late getting back to the diner. I'm outta here!"

The men drifted back to work, leaving Hannah a clear view of Jordan. He stood by an upright support post, staring morosely at his thumb.

"Can I see?" Kevin asked, and Hannah resisted the urge

to tell him to leave Jordan alone, because she knew how entertaining something yucky like an injured thumb was to a six-year-old boy.

Jordan held out the thumb solemnly, and Kevin leaned forward to inspect it.

"Not much blood," he said in disappointment. "I cut my knee once and, man, I bet there was gallons of blood."

"Look at this," Jordan told him, pulling up his shirt to display a small scar on his ribs. "I fell off my bike once."

"Heck, I fall off my bike all the time," Kevin said with a shrug. "Especially if I'm trying to do wheelies."

"This is a big bike," Jordan told him. "A motorcycle."

"You got a motorcycle?" Kevin asked, his eyes wide.

Esther honked the VW's horn, and Hannah decided it was time to put an end to the display of machismo on the part of both males.

"If you boys are through trading war stories," she said, "Esther is waiting."

"'Bye, Mom!" Kevin called as he bolted for the car.

Hannah carefully tried to keep her eyes away from Jordan's chest, which was still bared after his little scar display. But she had caught an eyeful of the dark hair and slab of muscles beneath, and she found that her pulse was thumping away in double-time.

"Nurse Hannah," he said with a teasing smile, "I'm ready when you are. What kind of first aid did you have in mind?"

"A tourniquet to your neck," she said dryly, turning and heading for the trailer.

But she didn't dare look at him, because she was feeling far less sure of herself than she'd sounded. She found the cream in the cupboard, then turned abruptly to find him much too close.

"Stand in the light where I can see," she told him, more to put some distance between them than as a visual aid. "It doesn't look too bad," she commented as he held up his thumb.

"I'm wounded here," he protested. "I'll have you know I put considerable force behind my hammer."

"A regular Paul Bunyan," she muttered. "The women must cluster around you just to sigh while you work." It was a mean-spirited thing to say, but she couldn't regret it. Not when she knew she was one of those clustering and sighing women.

"I've had my share of...admirers," Jordan admitted.

"Don't you mean lovers?" she retorted.

"I didn't always go to bed with them," he said quietly, looking into her face until she was forced to look away. "I'm not the playboy you seem to think I am."

Not if you don't consider dumping one woman when a better one comes along the actions of a playboy, she thought bitterly.

But she arched her brows and didn't comment. She ran the water in the sink until it was warm, then took his hand by the wrist and held his thumb under the running water. She could feel him looking at her, but she stoically ignored him. Instead, she rubbed some soap on two fingers of her free hand and began to lather his thumb.

"Ow," he said softly.

"I'm sorry," she said, looking up at him. "I need to clean it."

"It didn't hurt," he said, and when she continued to stare at him, confused, he added, "I wanted to see your face."

Flushing, Hannah looked away again, abruptly turning off the water and drying his hand on a paper towel.

Jordan remembered his brother Jake telling him that he was sure he fell in love with his wife at the moment she took a splinter from his thumb—but he hadn't recognized it as love at the time.

But love was not an entanglement that Jordan McClennon wanted, and he carefully reined in his emotions. It was one thing to build an emotional bond with a son, quite another to fall in love with a woman.

A son. It just couldn't be. He had never imagined himself as a father. It smacked of...too much responsibility.

With the blood washed away, Hannah could see that he had scraped the knuckle badly. It would be sore and bruised, but the damage was minimal.

"Lucky you," she said brightly. "It looks like your nail's going to be okay."

"Lucky me," he repeated quietly. Something in his tone unsettled her, and she frowned down at his hand as she dabbed on the cream. When she finished, she turned away and capped the cream, reaching into the cupboard to put it away.

When she turned back around he was too close to her again. She pressed her back against the sink.

"Hannah, you don't have to act like a scared rabbit," he teased her, his eyes studying her. "I'm not about to eat you alive."

"Yes, you are," she told him in all seriousness.

"What makes you think that?"

"Because you did it before. I was alone in the city in my first job and nervous enough about doing it right, when the great Jordan McClennon decided to have his fun. Oh, you wined and dined me and whispered sweet things in my ear until my head was swimming with the excitement of it all." She stopped to take a deep breath. "And when you'd had your fun with me, some other girl with long legs and collagen lips crossed your path and swiveled her hips, and you went chasing after her." He started to say something, but Hannah held up her hand to stop him. "It's all right. I learned my lesson the hard way, but you'd better believe I learned it, Jordan. I have no use for you or any other man of your kind. You think you're God's gift to women, and the sooner they unwrap the package the better."

For all her bravery, Jordan saw that her lower lip was quivering. He wanted to gather her in his arms and tell her he was sorry for whatever had happened then. He truly did not remember another woman, and he certainly had never meant to hurt Hannah.

The loan approval had generated a ton of paperwork, and he had spent the next two weeks at either the bank or the office of the economic development agency, filling out a completely new batch of forms in triplicate. And, somewhere in between, he had to meet with lawyers to insure that all of those triplicate forms were in accordance with federal and local business regulations.

Just after 7:00 p.m. on the fifteenth day of the process, after he had signed his name for the last time and taken three aspirin for a roaring headache—triplicate had become a habit—he had tried to call Hannah.

Her phone had been disconnected.

He'd broken one of his cardinal rules and called his personnel manager at home. He found out that Hannah Brewster had resigned and left town. She had left no forwarding address with either the company or her landlady.

Jordan had been dumbfounded, and then annoyed. His attentions to the opposite sex had never before had the effect of driving them out of town.

Now he thought that perhaps he understood why she'd left.

Was it because she'd been pregnant?

He could think of no other reason, and yet he couldn't find the words to come out and ask her. She was too defensive, too determined to keep him away from her, and if he asked now he was sure she would deny it, out of pride if nothing else.

But he didn't get a chance to ask. The door burst open, and Ronnie flew inside, holding his nose. He looked at the two of them. Then, apparently recognizing the tension on their faces, he started to back toward the door.

"What is it, Ronnie?" Hannah asked in concern.

"A bee stung me," he muttered through his hand. "My nose feels like a lightbulb."

Hannah was still shaking inside from her speech to Jordan, but she struggled to appear calm.

"Come on," she said, her voice even. "Let's take a look."

From the corner of her eye she could see Jordan moving toward the door. She refused to look at him. She had said her piece, and she was sure that he understood her position. He would be a fool to pursue her now.

As the door closed, Hannah mustered a smile for Ronnie and inspected his nose.

"Is Jordan giving you trouble?" he asked hesitantly.

Hannah shook her head. "We had an argument over something that happened a long time ago," she said. "Nothing more."

Ronnie looked unconvinced, but Hannah was determined that this was the end of all speculation about her and Jordan McClennon.

"There's nothing between Jordan and me," she told him. "And you can tell your mama that, too. St. Jude will have to find another victim."

And that, she hoped, was the end of that.

Three

Jordan sat back in his office chair and stared out the window. In front of him the computer whirred and clicked as it exited the document he'd been reading, the one that confirmed what he'd remembered.

"Personnel."

He'd found Hannah's name, found the date she'd left the company—with excellent references. And that date had come shortly after official word had been announced on the business loan that had financed the company's expansion.

So almost immediately after he'd wined and dined her, as she put it, and then made love to her, she had left the company. And Jordan had no ready explanation except that she'd been pregnant with his child.

You're in deep beef stew, Jordan, he told himself, echoing the words his mother spoke often enough to one of her three sons.

It had been four days since the revelation had hit him at Esther's house that he might very well be Kevin's father, and it had taken him all of those four days to get up the nerve to check the computer files.

He tugged at his collar nervously. What was he supposed to do now? Hannah didn't even want to speak to him again, and her son wanted a dad. Not that he was dad material. Quite the contrary. He'd known for a long time that he didn't care for domestication. He wanted his freedom. He didn't feel anything like a father. All of his life, he'd hungered for something that would be his alone, and his business filled that need the way no person could.

But on the other hand, only a callous jerk would discover he had a son, then do nothing about it.

He threw down the pen he'd been tapping on his desk and stood, pulling impatiently at the tie he wore. Suddenly the office felt too confining. He wanted nothing more than to get out of here. But it was only five p.m., and Jordan McClennon never left the office before seven.

Maybe it was time to do something different.

Jordan parked his car half a block from her apartment, spotting her as soon as he got out of the car. She was kneeling beside a wooden barrel outside the front door of the building, planting marigolds. For a moment he was so bedazzled by her cutoff shorts and the length of leg they showed that he almost forgot the present he'd brought. He reached into the car to retrieve it, his eyes still on Hannah.

She saw him coming and slowly stood, her hands on her hips.

"How did you find me?" she demanded as soon as he was close.

"I...asked Ronnie," he admitted. "He didn't want to tell me. He thought we'd had some kind of falling out."

"We did," she said shortly.

He didn't know what to say to that, so he stood there tugging at his tie.

"Is that supposed to be a peace offering?" she asked, nodding toward the package in his hand.

He'd almost forgotten he was holding it. "Yes," he said as he held it out, unable to think of anything clever that might earn him one of her smiles.

Hannah stared down at the small, plastic tool box with its toy hammer, screwdriver and saw.

"A rubber hammer," she said without any change in her voice. "I'll have Esther's house done in no time with a rubber hammer. Does it come with rubber nails?"

"No, it's for Kevin," Jordan said before he met her eyes and realized that she was teasing him. She started to smile, then caught herself, and he felt his pulse quicken.

"I'll tell him it's from you," she said. "He's at his guitar lesson."

She started to turn away, and he took a step closer. "May I...come in?"

Hannah's innate Brewster hospitality was suddenly at war with her common sense. Despite his trucelike overture, she was still determined not to let him into her life again.

"Hannah," he said, "for whatever I did when we were together before—and I honestly don't remember chasing after another woman—I do apologize."

"It was more like another woman dangling her implants in front of you," Hannah said, feeling jealous and petty. She sighed. "All right. I guess it's just another episode in the Brewster Sisters 'Bad-Date-of-the-Month Club.'" She picked up her trowel and the empty plastic flower containers and fished out her key.

He followed her into the apartment foyer, assuming he had just been invited in, though he wasn't perfectly clear on the point.

An apartment door opened a crack, and Jordan could see a woman with gray hair and dangling earrings peering out at him. The landlady, he assumed.

"You have a sister?" he asked Hannah as he waited for her to unlock her first-floor apartment.

"Had," she corrected him. "Marybeth got mixed up with a fast crowd. She died of a drug overdose."

"I'm sorry."

He didn't remember her mentioning a sister before, but then he probably hadn't gotten far enough beyond his raging lust at the time to ask. He started to ask another question, but she was disappearing into a back room. Shifting his weight, he stood uncertainly in the middle of the room, looking around.

It was a small apartment, but bright and clean. The kitchen and living room were one big room separated by a breakfast bar. Someone had stenciled a red and blue flower design at the top of the walls. It matched the big braided rug in the center of the living room's wood floor. A bookcase sat opposite the blue couch, its shelves sagging under the weight of a considerable library. More books sat in piles on the floor nearby. He made a mental note—she read a lot, and for all her skill with a hammer, she hadn't gotten around to building herself a decent bookcase.

She came out of the bedroom, running a comb through her hair, and caught him reading the notes on her refrigerator. She'd changed clothes, and he tried not to stare.

"Nice pictures," he said, nodding toward Kevin's colorful drawings dangling from small, round magnets next to the grocery list and the self-adhesive memo that sported a recipe for something he couldn't identify, though it was obviously rich and chocolate.

"What can I say?" she said. "Brewster pictures hang on the finest refrigerators around the country."

It was her subtle indication that she knew he was trying to score points, and he frowned. If he'd ever had a flair with women, he was either certainly losing it, or this particular woman didn't recognize a man trying his damnedest to impress her.

"Look," he said. "Obviously I haven't been doing too well with you. But I'm not giving up."

"Why not?" she demanded.

That threw him for a loop. No coyness. No "Oh, go

ahead and try again." She just plain wasn't responding to him.

But he sure as hell was responding to her. Looking at her in those crisp white jeans and green knit top, he could feel his hormones responding all over the place.

"Because I have this theory about what you're doing," he said, making it up off the top of his head. "I don't think you're really so set on never seeing me again. I think you just want to put the fear of God into me that you're serious. To make sure you've got my attention." He tried to see her face as she bent down to pick up her purse. "Am I right here?" he asked. "Because I've got to admit, Hannah, that you've got me worried. Hannah?" he prompted again as she headed for the door. "You've got my attention, you know."

He scooted out the front door just before she closed it, frowning at her as she locked it.

"So, where are we going now?" he asked, following her back out into the sunshine.

"*I'm* going to the grocery store," she said, coming to a complete halt on the sidewalk and nearly causing him to bump into her. "And I'd suggest that you go home."

"What a coincidence!" he said, catching up to her and matching his longer steps to hers. "I was going to the grocery store, too. I think I'm out of…groceries." After a moment's silence he added, "You're going to have to watch it, Hannah. You almost smiled that time."

She couldn't help it. She wanted to be angry with him, to keep him at a safe distance if nothing else. But she couldn't seem to manage it, not when he brought her son a gift and tried so hard to be with her.

"All right," she said, realizing that this battle was lost. "I will stop ignoring you on two conditions."

He looked over at her, his innate cockiness firmly back in place. "And what are those?"

"First, that you tell Esther and Ronnie that you have no interest in me and I have no interest in you."

Jordan's brows shot up. "Don't you think that will only renew their enthusiasm in matchmaking?"

Hannah shook her head. "Not coming from you, the man with a deep, abiding interest in all womankind."

He ignored her sarcasm and shrugged. "And what's the second condition?"

Hannah stopped walking and faced him. "That you don't so much as lay a finger on me."

Jordan took a deep breath and straightened his tie. "Never? Like until the end of the world, et cetera?"

"Right."

"I don't know," he said. "I think I need a modifying clause on that one."

Hannah thought a moment. "All right. The only exception being the unlikely occurrence of an invitation from me."

"Does it have to be an engraved invitation?" he demanded.

Hannah finally smiled. "I think my word will be sufficient."

Jordan slowly grinned. "In that case, you have a deal. When I get through with Esther and Ronnie, I'll have them convinced that I think you're the most undesirable woman on the face of the earth."

"Thank you," she said dryly. "Please don't compliment me any further by explaining how easy that will be."

Jordan's grin widened. "And I will not touch you in any way, shape or form. By the way, is blowing in your ear technically considered touching?"

Hannah rolled her eyes and began walking again. Behind her she could hear Jordan whistling as he caught up.

This was perfect, he thought. He would be able to spend some time getting to know Kevin without risking any emotional involvement with Hannah. In time he was sure she would lower her barriers enough that they could talk about his son—most importantly, the fact that he had one, and the fact that Kevin's father was now part of his life. But

Jordan was still footloose and fancy-free, able to come and go as he pleased. No restrictions on his life.

Perfect.

The whole evening looked a lot better to him now. He could even look around and enjoy the brick bungalows with their neat yards peopled with children out kicking soccer balls or teens sitting on front stoops talking on cordless phones. He even enjoyed the heavy, almost sensual scent of fresh earth turned over for backyard gardens. And the pungent odor of hot grease drifting from screen doors as suppers cooked.

He continued whistling until Hannah crossed the street at the next light and slowed to admire the boxes of bedding plants on display in front of the small grocery store.

It was an old-fashioned, neighborhood grocery store, the kind where he was sure the owner knew his customers by name. The two large front windows were spotless, the name, Bettleman's, stenciled neatly in blue.

Jordan watched Hannah pause at the pansies, smiling as she lifted a petal with one finger.

"Is that what you're planting?" he asked as he followed her into the store.

"Goodness, no," she said wryly. "Those are ten dollars a box. My budget runs more to marigolds and petunias."

Hannah started down the produce aisle, stopping to pick up a metal-handled plastic basket. She began putting oranges into the basket, then moved on to the meat counter where Jordan watched her order a pound of lean hamburger. The woman behind the meat counter apparently knew Hannah, and made small talk.

"Those look good," Jordan said, pointing to the Italian sausages hanging by strings inside the glass.

The woman weighing the hamburger smiled appreciatively at Jordan. "They're excellent," she said. "Perfectly spiced."

"Then let's have four of them," Jordan said impulsively.

The woman glanced at Hannah with her brows raised,

clearly under the impression that she was the shopper in charge of this foray, and Hannah shrugged in disinterest.

"And were you planning on using my kitchen to cook them?" Hannah asked him.

"I make great lasagna," he told her, realizing that his only way to wangle an invitation to dinner was if he cooked it himself.

She turned with her hamburger and met his eyes, hesitating. The woman behind the meat counter looked on in interest.

"I don't want you cooking my dinner," Hannah said quietly.

"Listen," he said, coming up with the only excuse he could think of on the spur of the moment. "If I'm going to convince Esther that we're totally mismatched and have no interest whatsoever in each other, I'm going to have to tell her that we at least tried." He raised his brows hopefully. "Otherwise she won't believe it can't work."

Hannah sighed. He had a point. Esther wouldn't consider her job done until Hannah and Jordan had shared a couple of meals before discovering that they were unsuited to each other.

"All right," she said, capitulating. "You can cook one meal—but just one."

"Wow," said the meat counter woman. "I don't know how you did that, honey, but any woman who can make some good-looking guy talk *her* into letting him cook is all right in my book. What kind of perfume do you wear, anyway? I've got to buy me some of that."

"It's called Not Interested," Jordan told the woman dryly. "It's for the woman who knows what she *doesn't* want. That's Hannah."

A flustered Hannah gave him a light punch on the arm, making him grin.

"Come on," he said. "I need some groceries here."

He proceeded to load down her basket, though he took it from her, leaving her free to peruse the aisles and watch him hunt down his lasagna ingredients like a general planning a military campaign.

And that was exactly what he was doing. He was campaigning to be let into her life again, and she wasn't going to allow it. She'd only do what was required to satisfy Esther's matchmaking efforts.

His hand brushed her arm once when he reached across her for a bottle of seasoning, and she felt her skin burn just at the brief contact. But he seemed not to notice her discomfort, and she was relieved that apparently he didn't realize how his slightest touch affected her.

At the checkout counter, Hannah took her oranges, bread and milk from the basket to pay separately, aware that Leslie, the checkout clerk, was as avidly interested in Jordan as the woman behind the meat counter had been.

"She's so independent," Jordan confided to the clerk, making Hannah flush.

As Leslie was about to total Jordan's groceries, he said casually, "And add on a box of pansies, please."

"You're *not* buying me pansies," Hannah protested.

"What did I tell you?" Jordan complained to Leslie, who watched wide-eyed. "If it makes you feel better, Hannah, they'll be *my* pansies."

"They'll look lovely in your office," she told him, determined not to give in.

Jordan only shrugged and began helping Leslie bag his groceries.

When they left the store, Hannah could feel inquisitive eyes following their departure. So much for her usual pleasant jaunts to the neighborhood grocery. She'd probably have to start shopping at one of the big chain stores now, or risk having to explain Jordan's absence every time she came back.

Even the stock boy, Calvin, was leaning precipitously far over the service counter to watch.

Jordan took her single sack and nodded toward the stacks

of flowers. "Carry *my* pansies for me, if you would, Hannah."

She was irritated enough with him to refuse, but she thought better of it with all those curious faces watching them from inside the store. She was a coward, she thought miserably, always too worried about what others thought to make a scene. And Jordan knew it.

"I liked grocery shopping with you," he said when they were back at her apartment door. "Really," he said as she threw him a sparing look. "What?" he persisted when they were inside. "You don't believe me?"

"I think it's a novelty for you," she said, setting the pansies on the counter and admiring them despite her resolve. "If you had to do it more than once every five years it would bore you to death."

"I'll have you know that I used to go shopping with my mother all the time," he informed her, pulling his booty from the grocery bags.

"Regular little coupon clipper, were you?" she asked dryly, watching him as she leaned against the wall with her arms crossed.

Jordan looked over at her, apparently surprised that she didn't believe him.

"Now that's boring—coupons," he said, shaking his head. "No, I tried to find all the neat stuff in the store that we'd never tried before. Then I'd take it to Mom and talk her into giving it a go. Sometimes I was successful. And sometimes I wasn't. But we never would have had Italian sausage if I hadn't put some in the cart. Or anchovies," he added, making a face.

Hannah smiled at that, and Jordan went on talking, pausing occasionally to ask where some utensil was, telling her about his mother, Elizabeth, his two brothers, and the farm he grew up on, until Hannah felt as if she knew his whole family.

She glanced at the clock as he put the lasagna in the oven.

"I have to pick up Kevin," she said, reaching for her keys. "I'll be right back."

"Italian or French dressing on your salad?" he called as she went out the door.

"Surprise me," she said. As if he wouldn't. Everything he'd done so far had been a surprise.

Hannah told Kevin that Jordan had dropped by just to visit, at a loss to give more of an explanation. Kevin took the news in stride, asking immediately if Jordan had brought his "bike."

"No," Hannah said. "And I don't want you two trading war stories again."

"What are war stories?" Kevin asked.

"Never mind." She decided it was better not to tell Kevin not to do something because it seemed to inspire the opposite behavior. Just like Jordan McClennon.

Maybe she'd found the secret to male behavior, she thought wryly.

When they arrived home, Hannah found Jordan putting the last pansy in the planter outside her apartment, and she frowned.

"What are *your* pansies doing in my planter?" she demanded as she halted beside him.

"Visiting?" he suggested gamely, standing and brushing off his pants.

"You get those out of there," she insisted, her arms crossed.

"Mom," Kevin said from beside her, "are they poison or something?"

She realized from Kevin's tone that he knew something was wrong, but he wasn't sure what it was. She simply didn't want Jordan McClennon buying her flowers or cooking her dinner or…touching her the way he had done in the past.

"No, they're not poison," she told her son, looking at Jordan so he would know that the pansies were still not welcome in her planter. And he wasn't quite welcome in her home.

"Hey, Mr. McClennon," Kevin said, "can I see your thumb?"

Jordan solemnly held it out, and Hannah felt a prick of guilt that she hadn't asked him how it was.

"Cool," Kevin said, surveying the decidedly purple color. "Look at my tooth," he advised, apparently thinking he had to show some body aberration of his own in exchange for the look at Jordan's thumb. Sticking a finger in his mouth, he pulled his lower lip down. "See?" he said around the finger that was now wiggling the loose tooth. "Gonna come out any minute."

"So I see," Jordan said, bending down to look and sounding impressed. "Do you get much money for a tooth like that?"

Kevin nodded his head. "A whole fifty cents."

Jordan nodded. "It used to be a dime when I was a kid. Inflation hits everything. So, do you like lasagna?"

"What's that?" Kevin asked.

"See," Jordan said over Kevin's head to Hannah. "You need someone like me to get you to try new things."

"Lasagna is hardly new," she said, starting for the apartment.

"Apparently it is to your son," Jordan pointed out. "It's a cross between spaghetti and pizza," he told Kevin.

"He won't eat it," Hannah told him in a low voice as she opened the door. The aroma that hit her was wonderful, but she resisted the urge to tell him so. "And he doesn't touch salad," she added for good measure. She was being spiteful, but she couldn't seem to help herself, she who had never said an unkind word to another living soul. But Jordan McClennon had changed all that.

Abruptly she remembered the present he'd brought for Kevin. He'd said nothing about it when he'd seen Kevin, no overt "Here, kid, help me score points with your mother." She got it from her bedroom and handed it to Kevin.

"Mr. McClennon brought you this," was all she said.

Kevin looked at her curiously, but he loved presents, and she watched as he ripped open the plastic and hefted each small rubber tool in turn.

"Hey-y, neat," he said, grinning. "Got anything I can fix for you, Mom?" he asked hopefully.

"Maybe we can do that shower head after dinner," Hannah said, remembering the job she'd intended to get done for two weeks now. "Now what do you say to Mr. McClennon?"

"Thanks, Mr. McClennon," Kevin said, grinning.

Hannah saw Jordan smile and realized that there were other things around here that needed fixing, like Jordan McClennon's effect on her. His gaze swung to her, and she looked for something else to say to cover her sudden attack of nerves.

"You've set the counter," she said in surprise. "That's Kevin's job."

"He gets a vacation tonight," Jordan said. "Of course he's invited to play us a tune on his guitar."

Hannah rolled her eyes as Kevin opened his guitar case, apparently ready to take Jordan up on his offer right away.

"Try to stop him," she told Jordan dryly. If there was one thing her son loved, it was giving impromptu concerts. But she liked hearing him play, rank amateur that he was. She liked everything her irrepressible son did.

Kevin sat on the floor, carefully picking out a tune, then strumming with great energy on the chorus. Hannah smiled as she retrieved glasses from the cupboard and poured iced tea for herself and Jordan and milk for Kevin. She saw that Jordan had already put the salads in place. When Kevin finished, she and Jordan applauded loudly.

"Know what it was?" Kevin asked.

Now was the tricky part, Hannah knew. But before she

could say anything, Jordan said, "It was good, that's what it was."

Kevin grinned. " 'Camptown Races,' " he said. "I'll sing it for you now."

He launched into the chorus with even more enthusiasm as Jordan lifted lasagna onto each plate and set them on the breakfast bar.

There was another round of applause as Kevin finished, and he jumped up to take a big bow. "Hey, that smells good," he said, running to the counter and making a show of sniffing.

"He still won't eat it," Hannah said under her breath to Jordan.

"Want to make any bets on that?" Jordan asked smoothly.

"What kind of bet?" she asked, still reasonably sure that Kevin's picky taste buds would win this for her easily.

"If he eats it, you two ride to Sandford with me this Saturday and back on Sunday."

"On your bike?" she asked with raised brows.

"No, Hannah. In my truck."

He looked so supremely confident that she couldn't resist. "All right," she said. "And if he won't eat it, you get to wash all those pots and pans you used cooking this."

Jordan grinned. "Get out your dish detergent, Hannah. It's a deal."

"Hey, what's the holdup?" Kevin called as he climbed up onto a stool and leaned down to sniff dinner again.

"No holdup," Hannah said. "Let's eat."

She sat down, and Jordan's shoulder brushed hers as he took his own seat. In light of their agreement she was sure that it was an accident, but she couldn't help the involuntary shiver that ran through her. But Jordan just smiled serenely and lifted his fork in a mock salute.

Hannah held her breath as Kevin punched at the lasagna with his fork and lifted a bite to his mouth. He downed it with a gulp of milk and then noticed the two adults watching him.

"Shall I make you a peanut butter sandwich?" Hannah said from years of practice.

"Why?" her charming son asked, forking up another bite and shoveling it into his mouth. He looked from one adult to the other. "How come you guys aren't eating?" he asked around a mouthful of food.

"Don't talk with your mouth full," Hannah told him, stabbing her own fork into her salad. "I don't understand it," she said into the lettuce. "He won't eat pork chops, he won't eat tuna casserole, but lasagna he eats."

"It's bogus, Mom," Kevin explained, which didn't enlighten her at all. "I like spaghetti and pizza."

She resisted the urge to tell him that lasagna was neither spaghetti nor pizza no matter what Jordan had said. But a Brewster was a graceful loser, and she let the matter drop.

Jordan, to his credit, didn't rub in his victory.

In fact, he helped her clear the counter after they were done eating and pulled her dishpan from under the sink.

"What are you doing?" she asked.

"Helping with the dishes." He was smiling at her, and it was all she could do not to smile back, despite her aggravation with him.

"Kevin, do your homework!" she called as her son retreated toward his bedroom. "I don't need your help," she said in a lower voice to Jordan.

"Maybe not. But I always take responsibility...for anything I've done."

He seemed to be waiting for her to respond to that odd statement, but she had no idea what he was talking about. A few dirty pots and pans weren't that big a deal.

Hannah shrugged. "There are clean dish towels in that drawer," she said, indicating the top one beside the sink. "Drying is usually Kevin's job, too. I guess he lucked out on everything tonight."

"Everyone needs a break now and then," he said, then fell silent as she began running water.

He was careful to keep a certain amount of distance between them while they worked, but occasionally she would reach over with a wet dish, and their fingers would brush. Hannah was afraid she was going to drop a dish, but she managed to finish the chore without incident.

"Can I watch TV now?" Kevin asked, wandering back into the kitchen. "I finished my homework."

"I've got a better idea," Jordan said. "Let's fix that shower head first. Go get your tools."

Kevin raced off while Hannah tried to deter Jordan. "I think we've kept you long enough," she said. "I can take care of the shower head."

"It won't take us any time," Jordan insisted. "Where's the cutoff valve?"

All right, she thought, looking into his blue eyes. *Let's see how long it takes you to tire of all this domesticity.*

"In the closet over there." She gestured toward the utility closet in the hall as Kevin raced back into the room.

She listened to them work in the bathroom for a while, their low, serious voices mingling, the younger tenor and the older, deeper voice. Finally, curiosity got the better of her, and she tiptoed to the bathroom door, standing off to the side where she could see them work.

They were engrossed in what they were doing and didn't seem to notice her presence. Jordan had taken off his tie and rolled up the sleeves of his dress shirt. His expensive shoes sat on her bath mat, and he stood in her tub in his stockinged feet.

Hannah couldn't keep her eyes from wandering over Jordan's bare arms, the forearms knotted with muscle under the sprinkling of dark hair. In the bathroom mirror she could see the reflection of her bedroom, and she flushed as she thought unwillingly about those strong arms lifting and touching her as he had made love to her in his own bed.

"Okay, let's see how it works," Jordan said, tightening

one last connection and stepping out of the tub. He turned and saw Hannah standing beside the door, and he stopped where he was, his eyes meeting hers.

He had caught her frankly assessing him, but there was no amusement in his face. There was only an awareness, the same that she was sure she mirrored. She couldn't seem to look away, her gaze drawn irresistibly to the blue depths of his. He was flame and sea at the same time, the blue heart of a hot fire and the cool depth of water. He was promise and memory in one.

It almost caused her physical pain to look away, but she did. She would do no one any good if she kept looking at Jordan McClennon like a man-hungry woman.

"Why aren't you turning the water on?" Kevin demanded curiously from the shower.

"I was just going to do it," Jordan said, a gentleness in his voice that was the last thing Hannah had expected.

He walked slowly past her, his eyes not leaving her face until he reached the closet, even though he had to walk backward a few feet to keep her in sight. She practically held her breath until he disappeared inside to open the water cutoff valve.

"Turn on the shower," he called to Kevin, his voice sounding muffled and strained.

She heard the water run in the bathroom as Kevin shouted, "Hey, we did it!" But still she stared at the open door of the closet.

What are you doing to me? she wanted to scream. *What do you want?*

But she already knew what he wanted. It was in his eyes every time he looked at her. And to her lasting dismay she had let him see it in her face just now.

Jordan stepped into the hall again, his eyes finding Hannah immediately. "Good job, Kevin," he said, but still he looked at Hannah.

When he stopped in front of her she felt her pulse quicken.

"Do I have your permission to touch you now, Hannah Brewster?" he whispered, no trace of teasing in his voice. He asked as if it were the most natural question in the world.

Hannah swallowed nervously. "No, Jordan," she said quietly. With those words, the spell broke, and she tore her eyes away.

She stared at the floor, keenly aware that he had gone into the bathroom and was putting on his shoes, all the while praising Kevin for his help. She hurried to the kitchen before he could pass by her again.

Hannah heard him tell Kevin that he would pick them up at seven on Saturday morning for the ride to Esther's. Then the front door closed, and he was gone.

Her body and her emotions were so frustrated that she could have wept.

Four

Hannah was dressed and drinking her second cup of coffee Saturday morning while Kevin watched out the front window for Jordan. It was a crisp, sunny day with fresh air blowing through the screen.

The TV was on, but he paid no attention to it. Hannah had already told her son twice to come back to the couch, that he looked like a pet cat she'd once owned, a cat whose squirrel hunting was done from the living-room side of a big picture window.

But Kevin laughed, realizing no doubt that this wasn't one of her serious I-said-so-because-I'm-your-mother orders. And Hannah knew that if she were younger and more foolish than she already was, she would be patrolling the window with her son. She was looking forward that much to seeing Jordan again.

And yet, at the same time she was dreading seeing him. She couldn't deny the sexual awareness that had passed between them like heat lightning two nights before. And she had spent two nights dreaming of what would have happened had she said yes when he'd asked if he could touch her.

His mere presence scorched her with primal heat, and she ached to be in his arms again. It took every ounce of her Brewster fortitude to deny herself.

"He's here!" Kevin announced. "Hey, Mr. Mc-Clennon!" he hollered through the screen. "Come on in! I'll buzz you!"

"Kevin, don't run," Hannah told him in alarm as he dashed for the buzzer at the door, nearly colliding with the couch where she sat in the process.

He hung out the open door, talking to Jordan before he even got all the way into their apartment. With no way to turn off her son's unbridled enthusiasm, Hannah took her mug to the sink and began carefully rinsing it out to show Jordan that at least one Brewster was unimpressed by his arrival.

When she turned around she found him watching her, though he quickly looked away and tried to make her think he was paying all of his attention to Kevin. But she had seen the way his eyes skimmed over her face and then wandered lower, and she knew that he'd been looking at her with a certain amount of speculation.

Hannah did her own looking, as well. While Kevin dragged Jordan to the corner of the room where he kept his action figure collection in a box under the TV, Hannah let herself catalog Jordan's appearance.

She didn't think he'd dressed to impress her; a business suit would be more his style if that were his intent. But his choice of worn jeans was just as impressive. His thighs tightened against the denim as he squatted beside Kevin, and his chambray shirt stretched across his broad shoulders.

Hannah pulled herself from her reverie and went to the window to close it. She had to stretch across Kevin who was sprawled on the floor taking out plastic warriors one by one. When she glanced back, she caught Jordan looking at her again, this time at her breasts which were taut against the fabric of her pink T-shirt as she tugged the window closed. Hurriedly she went back to her post in the kitchen, a safe distance from him.

"Are you ready to go?" she asked, picking up her purse.

Jordan cleared his throat and slowly stood. "Are you hungry?" he asked.

"No, because I ate breakfast," she said pointedly.

"Well, I didn't," he said. "I'm hungry."

"Too bad," Hannah informed him.

"I'm hungry too, Mom," Kevin said brightly, and Hannah sighed. It was some kind of conspiracy, she was sure of it. She went through a daily battle trying to convince Kevin to eat breakfast. She had even packed peanut butter crackers in her purse in the event he decided he was ready to eat when they got on the road. And he decided to be hungry now.

"I could make pancakes," Jordan suggested.

Hannah held up her hand. "I will make scrambled eggs and toast if you two gentlemen find that suitable," she said. Her look told them that they'd better darn well find it suitable.

"Oh, yes, that's fine," Jordan said innocently, and Hannah turned away from those smiling eyes before they beguiled her too much. "We'll stay out of your way," he assured her. "Come on, Kevin. Let's see what's on TV."

Hannah resisted telling him that Kevin's TV watching was limited to five hours a week. She wasn't about to get into the rules and regulations around her home, because Jordan was sure to try to find a way around those rules. The best option at the moment seemed to be to pretend she didn't know they were watching TV.

It was a very difficult thing to ignore, because Jordan found the remote control in record time—even for a man—and switched channels until he found "The Three Stooges." There they sat, man and boy, side by side on the couch, Kevin mimicking the way Jordan propped one ankle on his knee.

Kevin found it the funniest show he'd ever watched, and his bursts of laughter made her smile. When Hannah looked over at them, she saw Jordan smiling as he watched Kevin, and she suspected he was getting as much pleasure from Kevin's enjoyment as from the show itself.

"Hey, look at this, Hannah," Jordan called. "They're building a house."

"And not very well, if I had to hazard a guess."

One Stooge howled in pain as another Stooge hit his thumb with a hammer—Moe being the hitter, Hannah saw as she stole a peek. Jordan glanced over at her and caught her watching.

"He hammers about like you do," she informed Jordan.

"Did you hear that?" Jordan asked Kevin, ribbing him with his elbow. "Your mother just insulted my building techniques. What do we say to that?"

Hannah was then treated to several minutes of Jordan's and Kevin's impressions of Stooge sounds—assorted grunts, nasal whines and *nyuck, nyuck, nyuck,* all topped with Kevin's whoops of delight.

"All right! All right!" she protested. "I give up! I'm sorry I insulted your building talents."

They gave her a few more *nyucks* for good measure before Kevin was caught up in the show again.

"What's that?" he asked as some non-Stooge presented a business card to "the boys"—Hannah would never think of the Stooges as anything but boys—and Jordan explained about business cards.

"Hey, neat," Kevin said. "You got one?"

Jordan pulled out his wallet and handed one to Kevin, who read it slowly and carefully.

"What's that?" he asked when he couldn't pronounce *Industries.*

"That's the name of my company," Jordan said. "And under that is my title. It tells what I do there."

"Breakfast is on," Hannah called. "And I need anybody but a Stooge to get the silverware out."

She avoided looking at Jordan as he sat at the counter while Kevin got their utensils. He was far too enticing with his banter, his teasing smiles and his attention to her son. Not to mention his tight jeans.

So far he hadn't been scared off by actually having to participate in the boring details of daily living at her home, but she wasn't giving up on him. No, give the confirmed bachelor another round or two of humdrum domestic routine, and he would find someone other than Hannah and her son for his amusement.

When she finally got enough food into Jordan and Kevin—two more pieces of toast apiece, on top of the eggs and the first two slices of toast—Jordan decided that now they were ready to leave. With both males laughing off her warning that with all the orange juice they had drunk they would surely have to pull off the road before they got to Sandford, she let Jordan herd her and Kevin to his truck.

Hannah eyed the vehicle skeptically from the sidewalk.

It was the same truck with the camper top that Jordan had driven the weekend before. Somehow she had expected transportation that was...larger. Unless she rode crouched in the back inside the camper, she and Kevin would be wedged in shoulder to shoulder with Jordan.

Jordan opened the passenger-side door for them, and Hannah made a valiant effort to get Kevin to climb in first. He protested immediately.

"I gotta sit by the window, Mom," he told her as if she couldn't remember anything. "I get car sick unless I can see out."

She was almost willing to suffer Kevin's car sickness to avoid sitting next to Jordan, but she was ashamed of herself the next instant. She couldn't bear to see Kevin miserable.

Sighing, she climbed into the high cab and sat stiffly until Kevin was settled on one side of her and Jordan on the other. Jordan's broad shoulders crowded her, and his arm brushed hers every time he turned the steering wheel. His long leg was stretched out to the gas pedal, his thigh lodged against hers. Even through her jeans she felt every movement he made. Each contact with his firm muscles sent a shiver of awareness down her spine.

True to her prediction, Kevin was in need of a bathroom when they were only forty-five minutes out of town. Long past any gas stations, they were driving the two-lane stretch of the route, passing a landscape of fields, cows and woods.

"How far to the next stop?" Hannah asked Jordan worriedly.

"Thirty seconds," he told her as he pulled the truck off the road. She had visions of cockleburs and rabid wild animals and poison ivy, but she gritted her teeth and managed not to sound like an alarmed, overly protective mother as Jordan escorted her son to the relative privacy of the trees and bushes just past a wooden fence.

"Hey, Mom!" Kevin called as he came running back a minute later. "Jordan taught me how to pee on a tree!"

"Oh, good," she said without enthusiasm as both males got in the truck, grinning. "Won't that come in handy in the city?"

"What?" Jordan asked her as he started the truck again.

Hannah gave him a blank look.

"What's that expression?" he said. "You look...pained, Hannah."

She sighed. "I'm giving thanks that there's no snow on the ground, or you would have increased his peeing skills even more."

Jordan found that incredibly funny, and she couldn't help looking at him as he laughed. He had a heart-stopping smile, and when he laughed, his eyes were warm and inviting, like the waters off some Caribbean island or the sky on a summer day. She had lost herself in those eyes once, and she didn't think she had ever quite made her way home again. Some vital part of her had been left behind in Jordan McClennon's bed.

"It's obvious, Hannah Brewster," he said, still smiling and craning around her to wink at Kevin, "that you are in dire need of another man around the house."

"No, I'm not," she said immediately, despite her own growing amusement. "One of those creatures is enough." She affectionately ruffled Kevin's hair just to make sure he knew that she was teasing, and he grinned back at her.

"Ah, but another man would add so much—"

"Mess," she finished for him.

"I was going to say character," he said, pretending to be wounded by her insult.

"Character as in milk cartons left on the sink, dirty plates in the living room, wet towels on the bathroom floor," she countered. "Not to mention the toilet seat."

"Now, Hannah, don't go insinuating things about men and toilet seats or I may take offense here."

"Oh, I forgot," she said dryly. "You rugged types use trees instead of toilets."

Jordan leaned around her to grin at Kevin. "You know what I like about your mom?" he asked. "Her sense of humor."

"Yeah?" Kevin said doubtfully.

"What?" Hannah said to her son. "You don't think I have a sense of humor? Is that it?"

"Well, gee, Mom," Kevin said, drawing out each word as if buying himself time to come up with some answer that would appeal to a mother. "You're...neat," he said finally.

"Neat, huh?" she said, enjoying teasing him. "Neat like—'The Three Stooges'?" she finished on a rising note as she let the fingers of both hands run riot through his hair, disheveling it completely. As Kevin laughed helplessly, trying to evade her, she countered with Stoogelike *nyucks* and *woop, woop, woops*.

All three of them were laughing when she finally relented.

"Mom, you are so...nuts," Kevin said, still giggling. He

was trying to restore order to his hair, but it was obvious that he had enjoyed the teasing as much as she had.

John, Jake and Ronnie were already at work when they pulled into the drive at Esther's trailer. Kevin jumped out and ran ahead, eager to show them his new tool set. Hannah slid over to the door, then stopped, looking back at Jordan.

"You'll talk to Esther, won't you?" she asked worriedly.

"About her matchmaking?" Jordan asked.

Hannah nodded. "Once she gets something in her head, it stays there, so you'll have to make a strong argument against us as a couple."

"She'll be disappointed," Jordan said.

"She'll get over it," Hannah assured him. "I'm sure she'll get busy looking for a more suitable wife for the last unmarried McClennon."

Jordan looked alarmed. "Wife?" he repeated. "For me?"

"Surely you don't think she's going to let you off the hook that easily, do you?" She tried hard not to smile in the face of his considerable discomfort.

"Couldn't we just let things go on the way they are?" he suggested. "Just until the house is built. Frankly, I don't relish the thought of Esther's meddling in my love life."

"No problem," Hannah said dryly. "Just bring one of your innumerable female conquests up here one weekend, and Esther will get the message. Your girlfriend can buff her nails while she watches your magnificent biceps flexing in the sun, and everybody goes home happy."

"Hannah—" Jordan began, sure that he had just been insulted by her tone if not her words, but she was already out of the truck and walking away from him.

He enjoyed the view, his eyes lingering on her trim hips that wiggled just a bit in those jeans, and her cute little bottom. He was an idiot to have agreed not to touch her, but if he hadn't he was sure she would have thrown him out of her apartment on his ear. And that would have been a shame. He would have missed those smiles of hers.

Jordan thought of her laughing on the ride here, and it made him grin.

"You going to sit around looking goofy or are you going to work?" a voice demanded from beside his window, and he snapped out of his reverie to realize that his brother John was watching him with an amused grin. "Though she is worth getting goofy over," John added. "I'm speaking strictly as an objective observer, a happily married, objective observer. What's the matter, little brother? Isn't she falling all over you?"

"She and I do not get along," Jordan said, making John back up quickly as he opened the door. He figured that if he was going to have to convince Esther that he and Hannah had no interest in each other, then he'd better practice on someone else first.

"Oh, really?" John said lazily, his grin widening. "Like the proverbial cat and dog, huh?"

"Exactly." Jordan began striding toward the lumber.

"Be careful that you don't get your nose scratched, Rover," John called after him, laughing.

It wasn't his nose he was worried about, Jordan thought as he surreptitiously watched Hannah.

John was right about one thing—Jordan was used to women who were far more *compliant* than Hannah, and his frustration level was rising rapidly. It was especially galling when it was her son—*his son*—he was interested in. He liked the kid a lot, and he was determined to spend time with him no matter what Hannah decided. But he was afraid that if he confronted her about his rights as a father she would be even more recalcitrant.

Jordan put his frustration into his hammering, nailing the floor framing as Jake cut the wood. Hannah was apparently intent on keeping distance between them and worked as far away as possible.

They rested briefly at noon, eating bologna sandwiches from the refrigerator, when Esther apparently couldn't get away from the diner. By late afternoon Jordan had shed his shirt in the growing heat and was beginning to feel the day's effort in his shoulders and arms.

Hannah kept glancing at him and then frowning back at her work. She didn't want to admit it, but the ride here with Jordan had left her longing for a continuation of the camaraderie they had shared. It had been a long time since she had laughed with a man. It was a simple thing, but it seemed monumental when it was so sorely lacking in her life.

While she was being honest, she might as well admit that she missed the way his shoulder and leg had touched her during the ride. It had been almost…arousing. And now she was edgy and restless and determined to avoid Jordan lest he guess the source of her bad mood.

She would feel a lot better once Jordan explained to Esther that there was no hope at all of a match between them.

The VW roared into the drive shortly after three that afternoon. Everybody in the yard winced when Esther cut the engine but didn't bother braking and the car gently bumped into the tree at the end of the drive, sending the little troll doll dangling from the rearview mirror into a mighty spin.

"One of these days, Ma," Ronnie called out, "you're going to knock down that tree or leave your fender on it."

"Fender, schmender," Esther said, waving away his warning as she climbed out of the car. "I got something better to think about—namely a barbecue to feed these hungry folks. Ronnie, where's the grill?"

"It's in the shed, Ma."

"My son, whose stomach calls all the shots, didn't get out the grill?" she asked, clutching her ample bosom in mock horror. "Are you too ill to walk, Ronnie?"

"Sorry, Ma," Ronnie said sheepishly as he trotted toward the shed. "I'll get it."

"Hannah!" Esther called. "Come help me make the potato salad. Jordan, you come, too. I need someone to carry stuff.''

Hannah pointedly looked at Jordan and raised her brows.

"All right, all right," he muttered as he walked past her. "I'll talk to her."

"Now," Hannah said, having learned that with a man it was necessary to be time specific.

"Can I help, too?" Kevin asked, rushing to catch up with them.

"Hannah," Jordan said, stopping and running a hand through his hair, a gesture she was beginning to recognize as pure McClennon. It meant that there was more to come. "I don't know if Esther is going to take my word about this…development."

"Then you'll just have to convince her," Hannah said.

"Well, yes, I intend to do that, but you know, Hannah, it might be easier if you were to *help* me."

"Trying to weasel out of it already, McClennon?" she asked dryly. She knew that she was on dangerous ground here, but her own frustration made her reckless. She parodied him, one hand on her hip. "I could use some *help* here, Hannah. I don't know how to handle this, Hannah. I could—"

He interrupted her sharply, his frown conveying only a fraction of the irritation she knew he was feeling.

"I'll take care of it," he said with deadly calm. "And then I'll take care of you."

She didn't care for that last remark and shifted nervously as he stalked into the trailer.

"What are you guys fighting about?" Kevin asked anxiously, and Hannah tried to reassure him.

"Mr. McClennon is supposed to talk something over with Esther, honey. And he wanted me to help him do it."

"Why didn't you, Mom?"

She didn't have a ready answer, and her refusal to accompany Jordan suddenly seemed silly. She realized that punishing Jordan because she was attracted to him wasn't very adult behavior. And it set a poor example for Kevin.

"Because I was being hardheaded," she told him truthfully, smiling and patting his shoulder. "You wait here, and I'll go see if I can patch things up."

She could hear Jordan's voice as she approached the trailer. He sounded more than a little aggrieved, and it was obvious that he was discussing her. He spun around the instant she opened the door.

"That," Jordan said, pointing to her as she stepped inside and quickly shut the door, "is the most aggravating woman I've ever met. She's stubborn and pushy and quarrelsome, and if you try to put the two of us together you're liable to have a murder on your hands. I would rather go three rounds with a rattlesnake than tangle with her, and if you ever find *anybody* interested in courting her I'll be surprised. There!" Jordan turned and stalked to the door, glaring at Hannah. He brushed past her and slammed the door as he went out.

Hannah walked into the kitchen, trying to think of what to say to Esther who still stood by the stove, a wooden spoon in her hand, her mouth open.

"My, my, my," Esther said, recovering herself. "I'd say sparks flew."

"Like a match and a gasoline can," Hannah agreed.

"Now, honey," Esther said, putting down the spoon and coming to Hannah to pat her shoulder, much the way Hannah had touched Kevin. "He's just a little upset right now. Men are like that sometimes. Touchy as all get-out and yelling like a bull, and the next minute they're bringing you flowers and candy."

"I don't want flowers and candy," Hannah said stubbornly. "I want Jordan to leave me alone."

"Now, honey, you don't mean that. Look what a fine man he is. Hardworking, dependable, and I'd say he could win a handsome contest hands down. And don't try to tell me you haven't noticed his chest. Why, he could put some

of those stripper boys on my favorite calendar to shame.''
Esther wagged her finger at Hannah. ''And don't you dare
tell a soul I got that calendar. Picked it up in Las Vegas
when the DAR sponsored that bus trip out there.''

''The Daughters of the American Revolution went to Las
Vegas?'' Hannah asked, momentarily distracted from the
business at hand.

Esther waved her fingers in the air. ''Psshhhh. They went
to see Wayne Newton. I went for Tom Jones and the slots.
Had a great time. But that's beside the point. Your Jordan
would make a fine father for Kevin.''

''He's not *my* Jordan,'' Hannah protested. ''And he'd
make a lousy father! He fed my son chocolate pancakes
and potato chips for breakfast and taught him how to pee
on a tree!''

Esther shrugged. ''Sweetie, a lot of men wouldn't bother
to feed a boy or teach him anything. The way I see it,
you're already ahead of the game. Here,'' she said, getting
a bowl of potatoes from the refrigerator. ''You peel these
and cut them up. I'll make the dressing. Ronnie!'' she
shouted as she opened the door. ''You get that fire going
good!''

And that was that, Hannah thought. Esther was in charge
again, and apparently Jordan's disclaimers had had no effect on her. And now Jordan was mad at Hannah. Well, at
least he wouldn't be bothering her anymore today.

As soon as she carried a bowl of potato chips outside to
the picnic table, Hannah realized that she was a fool to
believe that Jordan was going to leave her alone just because he was mad at her. He was sitting at the picnic table,
his back to the table part, his shirt balled in his hand, and
even though he didn't turn his head she knew he was aware
of her every step.

''You need any help?'' he asked, and then before she
could answer he added pointedly, ''You see how I offered
my help just then without being asked? I wouldn't want to

make someone do all the work by themselves if I could do something.''

She got his point right away but decided to take the high road and ignore it.

"It didn't work, anyway," she informed him. "Esther is still unconvinced that we're a bad match."

"Just what did you tell her in there?" he demanded, turning around so he could frown at her.

"I told her I had no interest in you whatsoever and that you're an egotistical, short-tempered idiot." She hadn't said that precisely, but she'd intended to say it.

"Idiot?" he repeated irritably. "You told Esther that I'm an idiot?"

"Well, no, not exactly," she admitted. "But I wanted to." At least that much was true.

"And do you know what I'd like to do?" he demanded, rising suddenly. Hannah backed up a step, even though the table was between them.

"I have to go back in," she said vaguely, turning toward the trailer, aware that Jordan's brothers were openly watching.

Jordan was faster, stepping around in front of her and blocking her way. Hannah feinted to the right and found herself headed toward the small shed at the side of the trailer. It didn't occur to her until she had almost reached it that no one could see them from here unless someone was lurking in the back bedroom of the trailer, spying out the window. That thought left her both relieved and alarmed.

"Just what do you need from there, Hannah?" Jordan teased, following close behind.

Hannah threw open the small door of the shed, hoping to spot something useful for the barbecue, something she could pretend she was searching for all along. Her eyes fell on a long pair of tongs and she promptly pulled them out. When she turned around, Jordan was standing so close to her that she took an involuntary step backward and tripped over the step, dropping the tongs.

He reached out and caught her behind her waist, bringing her back in close proximity to his bare chest. Her hands came up to put more distance between them, but at the contact with his hot skin she froze, staring into his burning blue eyes.

"You don't want me touching you, remember?" he told her softly. "Tell me to go away, Hannah. I want to hear you say it."

She knew that it was his anger with her that was making him deliberately provoke her like this. But she couldn't find the words to make him stop. And she knew it was because she wanted him to hold her like this. She loved the hard feel of him against her.

Slowly she shook her head.

"Then tell me you want me to kiss you," he whispered, and she could see that his anger was gone now. In its place was the same need she felt.

Hannah saw the gentling in his face, but still she couldn't speak. Her fingers curled against his smooth skin, moving restlessly over his chest. Jordan groaned.

"You're driving me crazy," he told her.

"Yes," she whispered.

He smiled, and then his mouth was on hers, kissing and tasting and making her melt inside. She didn't try to disguise her own need, kissing him back with all the fervor of a woman who had wanted this for a long time.

His lips were hot and slightly salty as they molded themselves to her.

She had been expecting the same challenge in his kiss that she felt when he kissed her at Esther's the week before. But after the initial urgency, his mouth gentled, tenderly brushing hers, his tongue softly tasting her lips and then the inner recesses of her mouth.

Hannah moaned against him as his fingers sought her breast and stroked a nipple into voracious hardness.

He finally pulled away, breathless, and leaned his forehead against hers. His fingers moved up to rub her shoulders, his thumbs making lazy circles on her collarbones.

"I could make love to you right here," he said huskily. "Does that scare you, Hannah Brewster?"

Hannah's eyes drifted open, hazy with desire. "No," she admitted, then stiffened as she caught a movement in the corner of her eye. She turned her head just in time to see a telltale green uniform swish away from the trailer window.

"Oh, God," she moaned. "I think Esther saw us."

"Damn!" Jordan said. He glanced at the window and then looked into Hannah's face, lifting a tendril of hair with one finger. "I'll tell her it was my fault, that I caught you off guard," he said.

"Very gallant," she said, "but she won't buy it." Hannah knew that even a disinterested viewer would have seen how willing she was.

"We could go ahead and let her think her matchmaking is successful," he suggested, smiling lazily. "I'm not going to complain about keeping company with you."

"Keeping company?" she repeated dryly. "Is that what you call it now?"

"Call what?"

"An affair." She abruptly pulled away from him and bent to retrieve the tongs. When she straightened she saw that his eyes were glittering with anger again.

"Is that what you think I want?" he demanded.

"Isn't that what we were talking about?" she insisted. "An affair, a fling, a one-night stand. It's all the same to me."

"Is it now?" he said, obviously irritated. "And I suppose it's all the same to you which man is involved?"

No, it wasn't. She wouldn't even consider such an offer from another man, but Jordan was a different story.

But deep down in her heart she knew that she would ultimately say no to Jordan despite the temptation to be with him again. She had a son to think of now, and she wasn't going to set a fine example for him by running around with a man suffering from commitmentphobia.

"It doesn't matter which man," she told him. "I'm not interested."

"The hell you're not," he said, and for a moment she thought he might kiss her again to prove her wrong. But he didn't.

Turning sharply, he strode away, stopping once to call over his shoulder, "I'm not playing your game any longer, Hannah Brewster."

She wasn't sure exactly what he meant by that, but she assumed he was ending all efforts to chase and proposition her. And while that was what she told herself she wanted, inside she felt a dull ache that might have been mistaken for disappointment had she been a foolish, hopeful woman.

But Hannah Brewster was not foolish, and she was not hopeful, at least where Jordan McClennon was concerned.

Five

Hannah was dreading the ride home in Jordan's truck on Sunday evening. From the relative safety of the trailer step, she watched him load some tools in the camper back and exchange a few words with his brothers.

He had given her a wide berth the rest of Saturday and all day Sunday—to this point, anyway—but there was no getting around the ride home. She was desperate enough to ask Ronnie, but he had left early for St. Louis because he had to stop at an electronics supply store on his way.

Kevin came out of the trailer with his new tool set, Esther behind him, and Hannah moved over so they could pass her on the cement block steps.

"So," Esther said as Kevin raced toward the truck, "got yourself into a bit of a pickle, didn't you?"

"Me?" Hannah protested. "Believe me, this whole mess between Jordan and me is his fault."

"Oh, of course," Esther said sagely. "How silly of me not to see that right off the bat. All you did was ride up here with the man, then try to convince me that you think he's the most disgusting male animal to ever walk the earth and then kiss him out by the shed. It's obvious it's all his fault."

Hannah sighed. "It's kind of complicated, Esther."

Esther lowered herself heavily to the cement block beside Hannah and gave her a long, hard look.

"I may not be the smartest woman on earth, Hannah, but I think I can understand what goes on between a man and a woman."

"That isn't what I meant," Hannah said miserably. "He's not my kind of man, Esther, but I can't seem to help myself from...forgetting about that from time to time."

"He's a fine man to look at," Esther said. "Reminds me of my late husband when he was in his prime. Lordy, the chest on that man. You know," she confided, "that's precisely why I bought my male stripper calendar. That Mr. June bears a strong resemblance to the late Mr. Wardlow. Makes me think of silk nightgowns and perfume again." Esther fanned her face in a you-know-what-I-mean gesture, making Hannah laugh despite her misery.

"That's the problem," Hannah said. "Jordan makes me feel that way, too, but—"

"But what?" Esther prompted when Hannah stopped. "He wants you, Hannah. Of that I'm sure."

Hannah felt her face color. "But for how long, Esther?" she asked quietly. "He wanted me one other time, too. And after ten days he wanted someone else."

Esther sighed. "Men are like that sometimes, honey. They want someone, but they're afraid of wanting her too much. They don't like to give up that kind of control over their emotions. Oh, my," she said, rolling her eyes. "I'd better stop watching those afternoon talk shows before I start talking like this all the time."

"Thanks, Esther," Hannah said, standing when she noticed Jordan watching her. "I guess we'd better leave now."

"You just remember," Esther said, "those McClennon boys are rock steady. When one of them falls in love, he's in it for keeps. Don't worry, honey. Besides, we got St. Jude on our side." She winked at Hannah, and Hannah stifled a groan.

She gave Esther one last wave before she got into the truck, and then tried to ignore the pressure of Jordan's leg against hers. For his part, Jordan said nothing as he started the truck. Kevin looked out the side window and waved at Esther.

"Were you and Esther discussing anything important?" Jordan asked casually.

Hannah glanced at him, recognizing that he was far more interested than he was letting on.

"We talked about St. Jude," she said, deciding that it was enough of the truth for the moment.

Jordan gave her an appraising look. "You're not getting caught up in this St. Jude hobby of Esther's, are you?"

"St. Jude's neat, Mom," Kevin offered enthusiastically. "Really. I've been to see him."

"There's an idea," Jordan said. "You want to stop at the diner and see St. Jude in the flesh—or concrete, as the case may be?"

Hannah nodded. Actually she was a little curious herself about Esther's mystical patron of hopeless causes.

"Do we need an appointment?" she asked dryly. "He must be awfully busy."

"I think he can work us in," Jordan said, and she could hear amusement in his voice. At least his anger toward her had diminished somewhat.

"I *love* this place!" Kevin cried enthusiastically when Jordan pulled the truck into the Burger Haven parking lot a short while later.

Personally, Hannah didn't see a lot to love. She had eaten at the diner once when she'd helped Ronnie move some of his things out of his mother's house. That had been when

Esther owned a house instead of a trailer. When Esther's sister had become ill and required extensive hospital stays, Esther had sold her own house to help with the bills. Now that Ronnie was making good money, he had insisted on building his mother a new home.

Even more of the neon letters above the roof had burned out, she noted, and the cinder block building had the look of a poorly dressed woman who had stood in the rain too long.

"Come on!" Kevin called, dashing around the building.

"You be careful!" Hannah shouted after him, though she wasn't sure which of many possible dangers to worry about most.

Jordan kept a safe distance from Hannah, but that only served to increase her frustration with him. She knew that he wanted to touch her as much as she wanted him to, but he seemed intent only on fueling the tension between them.

"So this is the great St. Jude?" she asked warily when she rounded the building. A small concrete statue stood next to the trash dumpster, its scalp rough and pebbly where what must have been a concrete cap had broken off. It looked as if it was once a garden elf, now the worse for wear.

"Not *the* St. Jude," Jordan informed her. "Esther's St. Jude. There's a big difference."

"Go ahead and talk to him, Mom," Kevin urged her. "Tell him what's bothering you. It really helps. Come on, Mr. McClennon."

Hannah watched in bewilderment as her son led Jordan away. Since when had Kevin been so concerned about her private worries? she wondered. She supposed that lately her aggravation had been all too apparent, even to her son.

"This is not what I need," she said in the direction of the statue when she was alone. *What did she need?*

Jordan. But she wasn't going to get him, at least not on a permanent basis. She might be his interest of the moment, but give him a little more time to grow bored and he would exit her life quickly enough. And she wasn't going to risk her heart on any of his short-term propositions. Besides, the man was entirely too full of himself.

"Sorry, fella," she said, giving the statue an awkward pat. "I think this hopeless cause is so hopeless that even you can't salvage it." At her touch, a small piece of concrete fell off and plinked at her feet. Hannah sighed. "Looks like we're both a little ragged around the edges at the moment. Tell you what, you try to hold yourself together, and I'll deal with Jordan McClennon. Deal?" Hannah shook her head, wondering at her own sanity. She wasn't prone to talking to concrete gnomes or saints or anything concrete for that matter.

Still shaking her head, she went back to the truck to find Jordan and Kevin drinking chocolate milkshakes.

Kevin got out and handed her a milkshake as she climbed in.

"So, did you talk to him, Mom?" Kevin asked when he was settled beside her and they were on the road again.

"We exchanged pleasantries," she said vaguely.

"Well, if you don't want to talk about it, I understand," Kevin said, making her smile.

"The important thing, Hannah," Jordan said, "is that you talk about what's worrying you, even if it's to a concrete statue. It's Esther's own private therapist."

"Hey, McClennon," she said in a low voice, elbowing his ribs. "Are you sure you don't want to stop and have a few words with that concrete bridge abutment up ahead?"

He rolled his eyes at her, but she continued giving him the business all the way to St. Louis. When they pulled up to her apartment, Kevin was laughing and Hannah was more relaxed than she had been all weekend.

Jordan carried their small suitcase to the door, then put his hand on Hannah's arm to stop her as Kevin ran ahead into the apartment. Her skin heated at his touch, but she didn't pull away. When she looked into his eyes, she saw a restless energy.

"Would you have dinner with me tomorrow night?" he asked carefully. "Kevin's invited, too."

She could see by the furrow between his brows that he still bore some annoyance with her, and perversity made her hesitate.

"I'm busy," she said vaguely.

"So many books to catalog at the library," he said dryly.

"Something like that." She crossed her arms, refusing to be intimidated by his closeness and warm, male scent.

"I don't understand you, Hannah," he said in irritation. "We both know you want to go with me, and yet you persist in this stubborn act."

"It's not an act," she said. "It might surprise you to know, Jordan, that not every woman falls in a dead faint at your feet whenever you dangle an invitation in front of her."

"I'm not dangling anything," he said, the crease between his brows deepening. "I told you I'm not playing your game anymore, and I'm not. If you don't want dinner, fine." He shrugged and abruptly let go of her arm, then he turned and was striding out the front door before she could say another word.

"Way to go, Hannah," she berated herself under her breath as she closed the door. It wasn't that she didn't want to have dinner with him. It was just...

It was just that she didn't want to start caring about him, and every step seemed to bring her closer to that dangerous emotion.

Hannah didn't sleep well that night, and she groaned when her alarm went off the next morning. She knew her weariness had more to do with the fight she was waging against her physical attraction to Jordan than it did with the hard labor she'd done all weekend.

Kevin was moving slowly, as well, but Hannah managed to get him to eat a blueberry muffin and some juice for breakfast.

"You know what?" she said to him as she ate her own muffin. "I think we both need some new clothes."

"We do?" Kevin said. "How can you tell?"

"Because your pants legs end about two inches above your ankles," she said. "Have you been hemming those pants in your room at night?" she teased him.

"Mom, I'm growing!" he protested, but he laughed, anyway.

"Okay, here's the plan," she told him. "I've got today off, so I think I'll drop you at school, then drive out to the outlet mall."

"I don't got a sitter," he reminded her. "She's on vacation."

"I don't *have* a sitter," she corrected him. "And I'll be back before you get home from school."

"Can you get me some of those Batman underwear?" Kevin asked. "They look neat."

"Anything your heart desires, Caped Crusader," she said, picking up her purse and heading for the door. "Let's hit the road. To the Batmobile."

Jordan tapped his pen absently on his desk. He hadn't been able to concentrate on work all morning. He kept thinking of Hannah and Kevin and about Hannah's determination to keep him out of her life.

He'd told her he wasn't playing her game anymore, and he had meant it. Now he had to show her he meant it. He wasn't going to be excluded from his son's life, even if Hannah wasn't going to acknowledge that Kevin was his son.

He had never thought that he would enjoy children. They were noisy and demanding and mischievous. He liked his brothers' children, but he wasn't around them very much.

So he wasn't at all prepared for the discovery that he actually liked Kevin. More than that, he had fun with the boy. He wasn't sure if it was because Kevin was his son or because he liked Kevin's mother. But whatever the cause, he was surprised at his own depth of feeling.

Now, if he could just get around the obstacles that Kevin's annoying mother kept throwing in his path. He was going to have to confront her at some point about his son, but she was so independent that he would have to find exactly the right moment.

The phone on his desk rang, and he picked it up, still seeing the images of Hannah and Kevin in his mind.

"Mr. McClennon?" a woman's voice asked hesitantly. "I'm Mrs. Peterson—Claire Peterson, the secretary at Rosewood Elementary."

"Yes?" He dragged himself from his reverie and tried to figure out why this woman was calling him.

"Kevin's school," she prodded him. "Kevin's ill and we can't reach his mother. He asked that we call you, and although you aren't officially on his records I—" The woman cleared her throat.

"Kevin's sick?" Jordan asked, frowning. "What's wrong? Does he need a doctor?"

"No, Mr. McClennon," Mrs. Peterson assured him. "There's no need to panic. This bug has been going around lately. It's just that we can't keep him here at school when he's sick. We just don't have the facilities. And, I know this is forward of me, but since we can't reach his mother…"

"You want me to come get him?" Jordan asked, when she faltered to a stop again.

"Well, yes, I mean if that's—" He heard the woman sigh. "I'm sorry, Mr. McClennon. Your living arrangement isn't very unusual in this day and age, and I don't know why Ms. Brewster didn't give us some indication."

"Indication of what, Mrs. Peterson?" Jordan asked, baffled.

"That you two are…living together," the woman said, clearing her throat again.

"Living together," Jordan repeated.

"Kevin told me that you're his new father. And he had your business card in his pocket. Really, Mr. McClennon, there's nothing to be embarrassed about. This happens all the time. These kind of living arrangements," she added hastily. "I hesitated to call you, but I recognized your name. I know that you're a responsible adult and not just some—" The throat clearing began again.

"Mrs. Peterson, Hannah Brewster and I are not—" Jordan began, then abruptly stopped. There was no harm in letting Mrs. Peterson feed her domestic fantasies where he and Hannah were concerned. Besides, this could work to his advantage.

"Not what, Mr. McClennon?" Mrs. Peterson asked.

"We're not formally living together," Jordan said smoothly. "But we do have a relationship, so in a way I guess I *am* Kevin's father. And I'll be right there to pick him up. Thank you for calling, Mrs. Peterson. Hannah and I are both concerned about Kevin's welfare."

There, he thought when he hung up. That should do it. Now he would have some leverage with Hannah.

Jordan quickly arranged for his assistant to cancel two unimportant meetings he had scheduled that afternoon and said he wouldn't be back until morning.

Jordan managed to escape the school office with Kevin in tow and without having to exchange more than a few more words with Mrs. Peterson, who had turned out to be a curly haired blonde with thick makeup and more than a passing interest in his love life.

When he had settled a pale, somber Kevin in the front seat of the truck, Jordan climbed in the driver's side and faced the boy.

"You know, there's something we have to talk about, don't you?" Jordan asked gently. "And we'd better do it before your mother comes down hard on both of us."

"Yes, Mr. McClennon," Kevin said quietly. "I know I shouldn'ta told people you're my father." He lifted worried eyes to Jordan's face. "It's just that I've been wanting a father for so long, and Mom never does anything about it, and then I talked to St. Jude, and I asked for you to be my father, and—" Kevin stopped talking, winded, and sighed. "I guess I made a mess of things. Mrs. Peterson's gonna tell everyone. I just know it. Just like she's gonna tell 'em I throwed up on her desk."

Jordan couldn't help smiling. He could remember so many youthful confessions he'd had to make to his mother. And Kevin sounded as sorrowful as he'd been at the time.

"It's all right," he said, reaching out to rub Kevin's shoulder. "I think I might enjoy being your dad. But there's something else."

Kevin brightened immediately. "You mean you'd really be my dad and come to parents' night at school next fall and my guitar recital and all that stuff? And my class picnic? Oh, wow, I hope I'm not sick on the day of the picnic."

"I think I could manage those things," Jordan assured him, laughing. "But you have to do something for me."

"What? I'll do anything."

"Do you think you could call me Jordan instead of Mr. McClennon?"

"Oh, sure, Mr.—Jordan!" Kevin said quickly, a grin breaking out across his face.

"All right," Jordan said, starting the truck. "Let's get you home."

"Jordan?" Kevin asked tentatively. "Could you do one more thing?"

"If I can."

"Could you take me for a ride on your motorcycle?"

Jordan grinned. "Sure thing. As soon as you're well." Jordan thought of one more matter he needed settled. "Kevin," he said, "you have a key to your apartment, don't you?"

"Oh, sure," Kevin told him. "It's here in the side of my sneaker so I don't lose it."

"Great," Jordan said, satisfied. "We won't have to do any explaining to the landlady."

Hannah started to insert her key in her apartment lock, then stopped when she heard something inside. It sounded like the TV. Actually, it sounded like "The Three Stooges" on TV.

Frowning, she quietly unlocked the door and eased it open, ready to run if need be. The moment her eyes lighted on Jordan in the kitchen, she said, "What—" but he cut her off, raising a finger to his lips and nodding toward the living room.

Kevin was asleep on the couch, cradling a pillow. Someone—Jordan, she supposed—had covered him with an afghan. "The Three Stooges" cavorted across the TV screen, bashing each other with large boards.

Jordan's suit coat lay over a chair, and when she looked back at him she realized that he must have been at his office. He was wearing a crisp white, long-sleeved shirt and charcoal pants. He still wore his red tie, though it was loosened.

Hannah quickly closed the door, deposited her shopping bags on the floor and motioned for Jordan to follow her to the bedroom. She closed the door and rounded on him. "*What* are you doing here?" she demanded in a loud whisper. "And why is Kevin home?" She glanced at the closed door, her face worried.

"Kevin got sick at school," he said, his eyes roving over her face and then lower. "He's just got a bug, nothing serious. But they had to send him home. A Mrs. Peterson called me to pick him up."

"And why would she call you?"

"Ah, well, that's a good question." He was smiling crookedly, his gaze on her legs now. She was wishing she'd worn slacks instead of a summery pink dress.

"Yes, it's a damn good question, and I want an answer. And stop looking at me!"

Jordan feigned innocence. "How can I answer your question if I can't see your reaction?"

"It's not my reaction you're looking at," she countered. "Now give me some answers."

He wasn't very good at appearing contrite. For one thing, that smile kept escaping. But at least he was watching her eyes now, which she found almost as disturbing as having him check out her legs.

"Mrs. Peterson called me because she couldn't reach you," Jordan said.

"But why *you?*" Her frown deepened.

"You see, there's been a little mix-up at the school," he began, pausing to gauge her reaction before he continued. "Kevin led Mrs. Peterson to believe that you and I were…" He cleared his throat, finding new sympathy for Mrs. Peterson's dilemma when she phoned him. He decided it was better just to come out with it. "Actually, Kevin told her that I'm his new daddy." He was having some trouble concentrating on telling her the truth, when what he wanted to do was stare at her in that dress. She looked so pretty.

"He *what?*" Her voice had risen way beyond a whisper, and Jordan quickly pressed two fingers to her lips. She looked so shocked that he thought she might fall backward, and he put his other hand on her shoulder.

"Now don't go ballistic on me here, Hannah. I took care of it." She didn't look very reassured. In fact, he thought that she still looked shocked. Gently he led her to the bed and pressed on her shoulder until she sat down.

"He told Mrs. Peterson that?" she asked, and when he nodded she dropped her head to her hands and groaned.

"Hannah, there's more," he said uncomfortably. He had thought he would enjoy irritating her with this new development, but he wasn't enjoying it at all. To his amazement he wanted to reassure her that he would make it all right.

"Oh, Lord, if there's more, I might as well hear it now," she said, lifting her head and pushing one hand through her hair. "Although I can't imagine how it could be worse than

Mrs. Peterson thinking that you and I are..." Her voice trailed off, and she looked at him in alarm, so much alarm that he sat down beside her and reached for her hand. "She doesn't think we're married, does she?" Hannah asked in horror.

"No," he said dryly. "Just living in sin. I corrected her on that. I'm not sure she believed me, though."

"Great," Hannah said, shaking her head. "Just great. All right, Jordan. What's the rest of the bad news?"

"I sort of promised Kevin that I would substitute as his father at school events." He braced himself, but she only gave him an incredulous look. "Like the school picnic," he added.

He was a little irritated himself that the incredulous look was still firmly in place.

"Why on earth would you do that?" she asked.

"Because he wants me to," he said defensively, thinking that now was the time for her to tell him that Kevin was his son.

He waited, but the moment passed without her saying the words.

"Well," she said, sighing, "the picnic is a week from Friday. I guess you can play daddy for eleven days."

It was clear from her voice that she expected he couldn't make it any longer than that, and her low opinion of him annoyed him even more.

"Look, Hannah, it was your son's idea," he snapped. "Maybe he needs a little more parenting than he's been getting from you." He knew he'd hit a sore spot the minute the words were out of his mouth, but he wasn't going to apologize now. She'd needled him enough about his intentions and what she considered his skirt-chasing life-style. "It won't hurt Kevin to have a man around," he told her, as close as he could come to calling a truce.

"I don't want my son using you as a role model," she told him bluntly. "I know I can't be a father to him, but I don't think you can be much of one, either."

"Well," he said wryly, "at least we know where we stand." So that was why she hadn't told him about Kevin, he decided. She thought that no father at all was a better option than Jordan McClennon.

Jordan sighed. So they were back to square one. Or maybe a little better than that. He had at least made his way into the tight family unit of mother and child that Hannah protected so fiercely. He would be able to see Kevin now, though he hadn't won any points with Kevin's mother.

They both sat in silence for a moment, and Jordan took the chance to look around Hannah's bedroom surreptitiously.

Like the rest of her apartment, it was a warm, relaxing room. The walnut chest of drawers was topped with a lace runner and a wooden bowl filled with pinecones. It was a woman's room, from the lace curtains and blue-and-white valance to the matching bedspread. His mother had had a small sewing room when he was a boy, he remembered, and it looked a great deal like this.

"I'd better check on Kevin," Hannah said as she stood. She sounded tired, and Jordan didn't stop to think when he reached out and caught her hand.

He remembered her insistence that he not touch her unless invited, but she wasn't objecting at the moment. She just stood there looking lost and bereft.

"Hannah," he said, standing, "I know that you're not putting up a fuss—well, not too much of a fuss—about me spending time with Kevin because Kevin wants it." He found himself looking into her eyes and wishing he could erase some of her worry. "But it would help if it was what you wanted, too."

"Whom would it help?" she asked quietly. "Kevin or you?"

"Me," he admitted. "But Kevin, as well. Hasn't he ever talked to you about wanting...a father?"

He had almost said *his* father, but he didn't want her to start slamming doors on him again.

"A father isn't something you can pick up at the outlet mall," she said quietly, her eyes fixed on his.

"Yeah, well, sometimes you can if you go to the right stores," he told her, relieved when she gave a half smile. "Hannah." He drew her closer to him, close enough to smell the sweet scent of her. "I won't hurt Kevin. I promise you that."

He saw the unspoken question in her eyes. But would he hurt her again? Jordan wanted to give her all the reassurance he could, but he sensed that it wasn't enough. Words couldn't convince her anymore.

Jordan brought her head to his shoulder and stroked her hair. He smiled, thinking how much he liked her short, sassy haircut. He liked everything about her.

Hannah sighed softly against his shoulder, and he liked that too. "Let me look at your face," he whispered, tilting her chin with his fingers. "I want to see how aggravated you are."

"Very," she assured him, but her voice trembled. Still, she didn't turn away, but let him look into her eyes.

She was so pretty, Jordan thought again. He liked teasing her, and he liked looking at her, and he definitely liked touching her. Her lips were slightly parted, her gaze unwavering. It wasn't that he thought consciously of kissing her. It was just that it didn't seem possible at the moment not to do it.

Hannah sighed softly against his mouth as it covered her own. If he hadn't told her he wanted her to sanction his new relationship with her son, if he hadn't looked into her face to see how aggravated she was, if he hadn't caught her hand, if he hadn't done any of those things, she might have been able to resist him now. But he had shown far more kindness than she'd expected from him, and it had thrown her off balance. It had made her feel warm inside, and it had made her think how lonely she was sometimes with no man in her life.

Jordan still held her hand, and he drew it to his chest, pressing her palm against his heart, so that she felt the heavy, quickened beat. His other hand found her breast, his fingers stroking so that she gave a short gasp of pleasure against his mouth.

She was kissing him back with all the need she'd kept bottled inside. The clean, male scent of him, the hard pressure of his lips on hers, the steely muscles beneath her hand—all made her head swim. She wanted him badly, and she was too hungry to pretend otherwise.

"Hannah," he said, his voice hoarse. "Hannah, I can't do this." He held her away from him, and she stared at him, still lost in a fog of desire.

"What?" she murmured, confused.

"I care about you and I care about Kevin," he said, his hands tight on her arms. "I can't do something I know you truly don't want."

Don't want? She couldn't believe that he thought she didn't want him at that moment.

"How...*noble*," she managed to say dryly as her reeling senses crashed back to earth. She had just made a fool of herself with him, and he was playing the knight in shining armor.

"Listen," he said gently. "You know that I'm not the type for a long-term relationship. I'm a poor risk for any woman interested in marriage. But I promise you that I won't let Kevin down. All right?"

"Marriage?" she repeated sharply. "I don't remember proposing to you, McClennon."

"You didn't," he assured her. "But you're not a one-night fling kind of woman, Hannah."

"That wasn't your opinion before," she said with more weariness than anger. She pulled her arms from his grasp and stepped back, her head high.

Damn, he thought. He wanted to take her to bed, and he

wanted to look after her and Kevin, and he was stumbling over roadblocks at every turn, not the least of which was his unappreciated sense of chivalry.

"I'd like to change my clothes now," she said quietly, "and then check on my son."

Jordan nodded and walked to the door. At least he would be able to spend time with his son. But as he glanced back at her composed face, even that didn't seem like enough now.

Six

Hannah tried to collect herself as she changed into jeans and a black T-shirt. She was still shaking inside from Jordan's kiss, but she had worked hard to hide it.

The last thing she wanted was to fall for him again, not when he was at least honest about his penchant for the single life. But she was afraid she was doing just that, falling for a man who would never settle down, who would always be eyeing the next pretty skirt to pass by.

When she stepped into the kitchen, Kevin was awake.

"I threw up in school, Mom," he announced enthusiastically. "But Jordan thinks I'll be all right in time for the school picnic. He's going with us."

Hannah glanced sharply at Jordan who was sitting on a stool at the breakfast bar, then sat down by Kevin to feel his forehead. "You're a little warm," she said, frowning.

"I took his temperature as soon as we got here," Jordan told her. "He's up a little to ninety-nine. I gave him some canned chicken broth and some ginger ale. He kept it down okay.''

"I didn't have any ginger ale,'' she said.

"I called the store,'' he countered. "They were happy to deliver.''

Wonderful, she thought. Now everyone at the school *and* the store assumed she was cohabiting with Jordan McClennon.

"Did you get my Batman underwear, Mom?'' Kevin asked, sitting up.

"Yes, honey, I got your Batman underwear,'' she said, smiling. "It's in the bag.''

"Can I see?'' Kevin asked.

Sick or not, Batman underwear was a matter of grave importance to her son. Hannah supposed that Kevin's superheroes took the place of his missing father.

"Nice choice,'' Jordan said from the counter, holding up the package of underwear he'd pulled from a bag. "Your basic blue-and-white crime fighter and sidekick.'' He tossed the package to Hannah who held it out to Kevin.

"Yeah, neat,'' Kevin said appreciatively. "Is your underwear like this?'' he asked Jordan.

"Ah, no,'' Jordan said.

Kevin nodded. "I guess when you get old you got different stuff on your underwear. And ladies got dumb stuff like flowers and hearts,'' he added, rolling his eyes.

"Or lace,'' Jordan said, sounding distracted.

Hannah glanced back at him, coming to immediate attention when she saw the pair of pink satin panties spilling out of the shopping bag onto the counter and Jordan with his head bent, trying hard to see what else was inside.

"Do you mind?'' she said through her teeth, hurrying to the counter and snatching away the panties.

"Is that a new nightie?'' Jordan asked, reaching into the bag and tugging out a short, sapphire blue nightgown that was as much lace as satin. He didn't seem the least abashed by her outrage.

"Jordan!" she cried in dismay as she grabbed the lingerie from him, too, then snatched away the shopping bag. "How would you like it if I went riffling through your underwear?"

"It's not half as interesting as yours," he assured her.

"That's not the point. I'm talking about privacy here."

"Then why do you buy underwear like that if no one else is going to see it?" he demanded.

She started to say that she bought it because she liked lace and frills, that pretty underwear made her feel feminine. But she didn't tell him that. He would probably conclude that her taste for sexy underwear was one of her methods for dealing with a decided lack of male attention.

Not that men weren't interested in her at first. But once they found out she had a child, their ardor cooled quickly.

She hadn't had a child when she'd first met Jordan. And she wasn't in the habit of wearing lace and satin then. Remembering that he had seen her underwear in the past—when he made love to her—made Hannah flush.

"One of my friends at work gave me some frilly...underthings on my birthday one time," she said hesitantly.

"And you liked them," Jordan finished for her. "Isn't that what we're supposed to do, Hannah?" he asked gently. "Buy things we like? Things that make us happy."

She didn't know anymore. She had a sinking feeling that what would make her happy was not within her reach.

"You haven't done that for a long time, have you, Hannah?"

He was standing close to her, his face and voice so gentle that she wanted to lean against him, to have him take her into his arms. She glanced quickly at Kevin and saw that he was watching with rapt interest.

"I'm very happy," she insisted. "I don't need a new thrill every other day to keep life interesting."

Jordan smiled despite the obvious jibe in his direction.

"Life is just a bowl of cherries?" he suggested.

"With a few pits thrown in," she retorted, cocking her head toward him.

Jordan laughed, and Hannah was entranced all over again by the sound. She had a feeling that the woman who finally tamed Jordan McClennon would get enough thrills to last a lifetime.

"Now what?" he asked, the laughter still dancing in his eyes. "Why are you looking at me like that?"

"Like what?"

"Like you think I'm the embodiment of...impurity," he finished with a glance at Kevin and another grin.

"Because you are," she said. "I'm sure your little black book of women's names and addresses encompasses half the telephone directories of five states. If all men were like you, we'd have to lock up every woman under the age of sixty to keep her out of your hands."

"And why is that?" he asked innocently, the laughter still evident in his expression.

"Because," she said, caught up in his amusement despite herself, "you're the Great Bachelor."

"Oh, I am, am I?" he said.

"Yes," she assured him. "Something like the Great White Whale, only harder to catch. And not as waterlogged."

"I don't have a little black book, you know," he told her.

"Then your memory must be astounding."

"Why do I always get the impression that you're insulting me?" he demanded, crossing his arms over his chest.

"Because I'm the only woman who doesn't flatter you shamelessly," she told him, aware that it was probably the truth.

"A single man has no dignity around you, Hannah," he said ruefully. "But I don't mind." His grin widened. "Because you need me."

"*I* need *you?*" she asked, barely able to conceal her astonishment.

"Definitely," he told her, trying to tame the grin. "I happen to know that Kevin's regular sitter—the one who lets him watch too much TV," he added to show that he knew what he was talking about. "That sitter," he said significantly, "is out of town. And Kevin won't be going to school tomorrow."

She was silent in the face of his pronouncement. Kevin must have told him about the sitter problem. He was right. No available sitter. And since she had today off, she didn't have a prayer of getting tomorrow as well.

"I can stay home alone," Kevin offered hopefully from the couch.

"Not on your life, buster," she informed him. And that left her with a problem.

"I could help, you know," Jordan said, raising his brows.

"You have a sitter in your little black book?" she asked dryly.

"I told you I don't have a little black book," he said. "But I do have flexible hours." He glanced idly at the ceiling as if entranced by her light fixture. "I could bring my laptop computer over here and keep an eye on Kevin while you're at work."

"You can't possibly afford that much time away from the business," she said, frowning. When she'd known him before, he would never give up any more office hours than absolutely necessary. If he could have moved his apartment to the plant, he would have done it.

"I can work here," he said. "I can keep in touch with the office by phone. I've done it often enough when I'm out of town on business."

"Why?" Hannah asked suspiciously.

Jordan shrugged. "Because you're in a bind."

Hannah decided that she would have to take him at face value, though she doubted his motives were purely unselfish. But, for the life of her, she couldn't figure out why he was doing this, what he got out of it.

"All right," she said reluctantly.

"I won't throw loud parties and invite wild women here while I'm baby-sitting," he assured her.

"Are you sure?" she asked skeptically.

He smiled innocently. "I'll just order in my usual champagne from Bettleman's store and maybe some steaks and a few cigars."

"Jordan! If you so much as order a potato from Bettleman's I'll ban you from this apartment forever!"

Jordan grinned. "I've never seen you so panicked, Hannah. What is it about Bettleman's that worries you?"

"It's not just Bettleman's, and you know it," she informed him darkly. "It's the school and Mrs. Peterson and Calvin the stock boy and Leslie at checkout."

"And what about them?" he had the audacity to ask.

"What about them!" she repeated. "They think we're—" She abruptly caught herself as she glanced at Kevin and saw him listening avidly. She lowered her voice to a loud whisper. "They think we're…you know," she finished, unable to come up with an appropriate word that Kevin wouldn't understand right away.

"And what if they do?" Jordan demanded. "If they have the time to worry about things like that, then let them." He picked up his suit coat and moved toward the door. "You're a grown woman, Hannah," he told her. "You're old enough to make your own decisions. Kevin, I'll see you tomorrow morning."

Hannah stared at the door for a good five seconds after it closed. *She was old enough to make her own decisions.* What the hell did that mean? He had been doing nothing but trying to make her decisions for her since he popped into her life again. And now he was telling her not to worry if everyone she knew thought that she was living with Jordan McClennon.

The man was impossible.

She looked at Kevin and sighed. "I don't know what I'm going to do about him," she said, half to herself.

"I like him," Kevin piped up, grinning. "He's neat."

And Hannah knew that she would put up with Jordan's aggravations for that reason, if for no other.

But a voice in the back of her head told her that there were other reasons too.

Hannah took a deep breath as she stopped before her apartment door after work. Something smelled delicious, and the aroma seemed to be wafting from her apartment.

She rolled her eyes as she heard the now familiar *nyuck, nyuck* coming from the TV. Apparently, Jordan had located an All Stooge channel.

Jordan had been all business when he'd arrived that morning with his laptop computer in hand, shooing her out the door with assurances that he and Kevin would be just fine.

She didn't know what she expected to find now—something on the order of sugar-coated cereal and chocolate syrup splattered all over the floor, she supposed. Dishes in the sink and Jordan's papers spread across the living room.

But when she opened the door, she found the apartment as neat as when she'd left that morning—except for a large box sitting next to the wall where there used to be a bookcase.

Her startled eyes flew first to Kevin lying on the couch and then to Jordan, sitting at her breakfast counter, his eyes intent on the laptop computer. For just a moment she forgot about her bookcase, because Jordan looked so...so much the Great Bachelor with his white sport shirt and tan slacks, his muscular hands moving over the keyboard.

Hannah swallowed hard as she remembered vividly how those hands had felt moving over her.

Then she pulled herself together and shut the door loudly.

"*What* have you done to my apartment?" she demanded.

"Hi, Mom!" Kevin called from the couch.

Jordan looked at Kevin and grinned. "We're redecorating," he told her. "Kevin and I think a librarian needs a better bookcase."

"Oh, I can see that that's far better," she said sarcastically, nodding toward the empty wall. "I have tons of room for my books now."

"That's the problem," Jordan said unabashedly. "You see, I need a little help in putting it together. By the way, did I tell you how lovely you look today in that skirt?"

"Flattery will get you nowhere, McClennon," she informed him. But she felt her heartbeat quicken, because he was looking at her legs in a decidedly admiring way again.

"Ah, well," he said, raising his eyes to her face, "I'll just have to come out and ask. Hannah, will you help me put this bookcase together?"

She had a feeling that he could do it very well himself, but she liked the idea that he had asked her to help.

"Right after dinner," she said. "What smells so good?"

"Roast chicken," Jordan said. "I put it in the oven to keep it warm."

"You roasted a chicken?" she asked in amazement.

He grinned and shook his head. "They have this little roaster case in Bettleman's. Nice little thing it is, too. Filled with roast chickens all ready to eat."

"I know all about that little roaster case," she said, aghast that he'd been shopping on her behalf at Bettleman's again. "And I thought you weren't going to order anything from there."

"I didn't," he told her. "Kevin ordered it. He decided he's ready to eat some solid food."

"You should have seen the lady when she brought it," Kevin informed her enthusiastically. "She really looked glad to do it. She's that lady who always talks to you when you're paying for your stuff, Mom."

"Oh, good," Hannah said weakly. "Leslie."

"Yeah, that's the one!" Kevin said.

Hannah shot a dark look at Jordan. "You're doing this deliberately, aren't you?" she demanded.

"Doing what, Hannah?" he asked innocently.

"Making sure that everyone thinks that we're…seeing each other." She had started to say "living together" instead but censored herself in front of Kevin.

"Aren't we seeing each other?" Jordan asked.

"No, we aren't," Hannah told him. "We're just…" She stopped, realizing that she was at a loss to describe their tumultuous relationship, which was more like a sparring match with a past history of lovemaking thrown into the mix. "We're just old friends," she said at last.

"Are we?"

"Yes," she said, deciding that she could let herself be friends with this man.

"Well, that's something," he said softly, and Hannah found herself mesmerized by his eyes, their flame-blue intensity holding hers. When she finally looked away, she could feel a change in the room—or in her heart. It was a change that she was at a loss to explain, but its imprint was there.

"All right," she said quietly. "Let's eat dinner."

Kevin whooped. "Boy, I've never been so hungry."

"I can see you've recovered nicely," Hannah said, smiling. It was good to see her son back to his exuberant self, due in no small part to Jordan, she recognized. She never would have suspected that the Great Bachelor could be good with a boy—and good for a boy.

Hannah hadn't realized how badly Kevin wanted a father, and it would have distressed her to know, when there was nothing she could do about it. Even now, with Jordan more or less active in her son's life, she worried about the loss Kevin would suffer when Jordan was gone.

But there was no point in anticipating grief before it hit.

So Hannah ate her dinner of Bettleman's roasted chicken and tossed salad that Jordan had put together from her refrigerator, and she tried not to stare at Jordan across the counter from her. Around his eyes were faint laugh lines that hadn't been there when she'd known him before. His face was older, more experienced. And yet it held as much fascination for her now as it had then. No, it enticed her even more.

Something was different about him, but she didn't know what it was. Maybe, she thought in bewilderment, it was she who had changed. Maybe it wasn't Jordan, but the woman who looked at him now who was altered.

"Ready for the bookcase?" he asked, and she dragged herself back to the present.

She carried their dishes to the sink, then followed him to the living room, still caught in her reverie.

Kevin watched them for about five minutes, then decided to go to his bedroom and read.

Left alone with Jordan, Hannah felt suddenly shy and awkward.

She stood, unsure of herself, while he pried the metal clasps from the box and opened it. He knelt on the floor, pulling out boards, then looked up at her.

"Could you get me a screwdriver?" he asked, his eyes holding hers. "And some wood glue, if you have any."

She moved away, feeling his gaze follow her as she retrieved her small toolbox from a kitchen drawer.

Hannah knelt beside him with the tools, watching him unfold the paper diagram and frown over it. His hands were large and capable, and even though he spent most of his waking hours working at a desk, there was nothing soft about them.

She abruptly looked away when she remembered again how they'd felt on her bare skin.

Jordan was watching her when she glanced at him again.

"The base goes on first," he told her gravely. "If you'll hold these two pieces together, I'll fasten them." His voice sounded unsettled, but Hannah decided that she was projecting her own emotional state onto him.

She held the two pieces of wood while he fastened them with the screws, and she avoided looking into his face again.

The whole assembly took less than half an hour and was accomplished with little or no talking. When the bookcase was done, Jordan lifted it into place against the wall and stood back. "That should hold all of your books," he said with satisfaction, stepping back and smiling.

"Jordan," she said quietly, "why did you get me a bookcase?"

His smile faded then, replaced by a pensive look as he met her eyes. "You needed one," he said.

"I know that." She waited, both of them knowing that it wasn't the answer she wanted.

"I like making you mad," he admitted at last. "And I figured a new bookcase would do it."

"I've disappointed you then," she said softly.

Jordan shook his head. "You could never disappoint me, Hannah. You're full of surprises, and I like that, too."

"Do you?" she wondered ruefully. "You've already told me that I don't know how to make myself happy by getting things I want."

"I was wrong," he said quietly. "I think you know how to get just what you want, Hannah."

She couldn't stop looking into his eyes. The blue color had softened, though his gaze was still piercing. She wanted to ask him so many things, but she couldn't find the words.

"Thank you for the bookcase," she said at last, recovering herself. "Believe me, I'll enjoy it." She managed to smile then, and she could see a change come over Jordan's face, as if he had been waiting for her to smile at him.

Jordan stood looking at her a moment longer, then bent to gather up her tools.

"I've got to check into the office," he said. "Do you want me to come by tomorrow?"

Hannah shook her head. "I think Kevin's well enough to go back to school. But, thank you. I really mean that, Jordan," she said when he didn't respond.

"I'll be tied up in contract meetings the rest of this

week," he said. "Are you going to Sandford on the weekend?"

Hannah nodded. "I have to take Kevin to the dentist Saturday morning, but we'll get there after lunch."

"All right. I'll see you then."

Jordan left after saying good bye to Kevin, and Hannah moved restlessly around the apartment, straightening things that didn't need straightening. She ran her fingers over the shiny wood of her new bookcase and then stared sightlessly out the window.

Jordan's words from a short time ago came back to her. *He wasn't going to play her game anymore.*

Then what was he doing? she wondered. She almost felt as if she were falling into some kind of trap.

Seven

Saturday afternoon Hannah and Kevin were almost to Sandford when she put on the radio for the news and heard the storm warnings. High winds and heavy rain, possibly with hail, were moving in from the west.

Hannah glanced at the sky, cloudy but not alarmingly so, and decided they were too close to Sandford to turn back. And summer storms rarely lasted very long, anyway.

Her eyes sought out Jordan as soon as she turned into the driveway, finding him working at the saw with John, cutting wood. He was bending slightly, his jeans tightening around his thighs and buttocks. He turned at the sound of the car, and even at this distance she could see how his blue chambray shirt turned his eyes an even more intense blue. Her heart gave an involuntary lurch, and she dragged her eyes away to check on the house.

It was progressing nicely, the walls and partitions in place. Ronnie and Jake were on ladders, installing the ceiling joists as they were cut. The house was going to look lovely with its backdrop of woods and flowers.

As soon as the car stopped, Kevin bolted from the front seat and raced to Jordan. "Look!" he cried excitedly. "My tooth came out!"

Hannah followed more slowly. She watched as Jordan grinned and stopped working to bend and inspect Kevin's mouth.

"Has the tooth fairy come yet?" he teased.

"Naw," Kevin said in a confidential voice. "I don't believe in that anymore, but don't tell Mom. Besides, it just fell out this morning. You think I'll still get money for it?" he asked worriedly.

"I imagine so," Jordan reassured him. "Your mom will tackle the tooth fairy and give her a thump if she doesn't." Jordan looked up and smiled at Hannah over Kevin's head.

"Worried about the tooth fairy finding you?" Hannah asked Kevin.

"Yeah, Mom, right," he said, rolling his eyes at Jordan.

Hannah gave him a playful swat on his shoulder. "Give your old mom a break," she laughed. "I like the tooth fairy."

Kevin relented, giving her an indulgent smile.

The sky was darkening noticeably to the west when they heard the familiar whine of the VW, its wheels spitting gravel as it came up the driveway. Familiar with Esther's driving skills, the group of workers stopped and collectively held their breath.

"Ten bucks says the bumper falls off this time," John said in a low voice.

"My money says more than six inches of tree bark hits the ground," Jordan answered.

The VW engine choked off, and the car silently rolled into the tree with a resounding thunk.

"For crying out loud, Ma," Ronnie complained from the ladder. "Haven't you ever heard of a brake?"

Jordan and John both walked to the tree. John inspected

the bumper, still attached to the car, then knelt and pulled a tape measure from his pocket.

"Only four inches of bark," he announced brightly. "It's a draw."

Jordan shook his head. "If she'd just hit it a little harder..."

"Hey!" Esther called, popping out of the car. "Any of you hammer heads hungry?"

"I am!" Kevin announced.

"Well, good, because I brought some fine fried chicken," Esther said.

"What happened to burgers?" Jake asked, climbing down from his ladder. "Not that I'm complaining."

"I thought you all might want a change," Esther said. "But if you don't want fried chicken..."

"Hold on, now," Jake told her. "Nobody said anything about not wanting fried chicken. You're so darned sensitive, Esther."

The last was delivered good-naturedly, and Esther gave him a playful smack on the back of his head.

John was kneeling on the ground near the saw. "Hey, Jake!" he called, "where's my drill?"

"Damn," Jake said. "I left it at the cabin. I was putting in a couple of new phone jacks."

"Better take Esther's car to get it," John said. "I've got both trucks loaded with new lumber, and it looks like the rain'll be here soon. We can't finish the roof joists without that drill."

"I'll run over and get it," Jordan volunteered. "I brought my bike today."

"You're going to get caught in the rain," John warned him.

"That's all right," Jordan said. "I'll take Hannah to keep me company."

Hannah flushed as Jordan's brothers worked at hiding their amusement.

"The cabin's as good a place as any to get caught in the

rain, right, Jake?'' John asked teasingly. Hannah saw the knowing looks exchanged between John and Jake, and her flush deepened.

"Can't think of a better place," Jake agreed, grinning.

"Can I go for a ride on your motorcycle?" Kevin pleaded. Jordan knelt down next to him and put one hand on his shoulder.

"How about tomorrow? It looks like a storm's coming right now."

"But you and Mom are going," Kevin protested.

"That's right," Jordan said. "This ride is for your mother and me. Tomorrow I'll take you on a ride all by yourself."

"Just me and no one else?" Kevin asked, his earnest face showing how important the invitation was to him.

"Just you and me, if your Mom says it's okay," Jordan told him. "And we'll stop for a milkshake."

Man and boy looked at Hannah, who nodded her head in approval of the plan.

"All right then," Kevin said. "You won't forget, will you?"

Jordan smiled. "No, I won't. Here, we'll shake hands on it. Okay?" He held out his hand, and Kevin thrust his smaller hand into Jordan's far larger one. Gravely, they shook, and Kevin nodded in satisfaction.

"Okay," Kevin said. Jordan stood and walked toward Hannah, Kevin watching them with a sober expression. "Mom, you and Jordan be careful now," he called after them, obviously repeating what he'd heard frequently from his mother.

When Hannah looked back to acknowledge his advice, she saw that the smiles on the faces of Jordan's brothers were kindly. She supposed that with children of their own, they understood the emotions warring inside her now— heady anticipation at the prospect of being alone with Jordan and guilt at leaving her child behind when he wanted to go, too.

"Here," Esther said, pressing a cardboard box into Hannah's hands. "Like as not, we won't be seeing you until much later. You'll need something to eat."

"We're not going off to war," Hannah protested, but Esther snorted.

"Knowing how headstrong the two of you are, I wouldn't be surprised," she said, wagging a finger at Hannah. "Now you be nice to Jordan, or I'll have to take up your case with St. Jude again."

Hannah clutched her heart in mock horror. "God forbid!" Jordan had wheeled out his behemoth of a motorcycle, and now Hannah looked at it skeptically. Had she really agreed to get on this metal monster with him? She felt as if she had just decided to ride a roller coaster—on top of the car instead of in it.

"How do you get on this thing?" she asked in a low voice filled with apprehension.

Jordan grinned and put a helmet on her head, fastening the strap beneath her chin.

"Just throw your leg over the back here," he said while he pulled on his own helmet.

"You didn't give it a cute name like Killer, did you?" she asked, trying to straddle the back without pulling a leg muscle. This was more physically challenging than her first ballet class as a six-year-old.

"It's a bike, Hannah, not a horse," he said. "Now hold onto me."

"Just try to pry my fingers loose," she muttered, flinging both arms around his waist, leaving the box of chicken mashed between her waist and his back.

"You just be careful, Hannah Brewster," Esther said. "You don't go fooling with the likes of a genuine patron saint if you know what's good for you." She leaned over to shake a finger at Hannah. "He'll bust your chops," Esther warned.

Jordan kicked the motorcycle starter at that moment, and

the engine roared to life, drowning out anything else that Esther may have been about to say.

Hannah was still musing over what *bust your chops* might mean as they left the driveway in a literal cloud of dust.

Jordan abruptly pulled to the side of the road when they were out of sight of the trailer, and Hannah found her heart pounding against her ribs in an agony of suspense. Now what was he doing?

But Jordan only reached back for the box of chicken, then dismounted, stepping behind her and tugging her forward until he had access to a storage compartment. He gave her a short smile and got back on in front of her, taking both her hands and placing them around his waist.

"The whole secret to riding tandem on a motorcycle is to stay so close together that the two riders almost become one," he told her. "Closer," he said when she leaned forward but still kept two inches between them. "You don't want to bounce off, do you?" he asked.

That was all the prompting she needed. Hannah immediately pressed herself tightly against Jordan's back, her breasts nearly flattened against him. She could feel his low laugh vibrate through her skin.

"That's better," he said.

Hannah's heart lurched all over again. She could just imagine Esther's pleasure if she could see the two of them now.

At first Hannah closed her eyes and let the breeze flow over her arms. But that made her all too aware of the sensations fluttering through her skin where she touched Jordan.

But with her eyes open she was even more aware of his broad, strong shoulders and dark hair. She longed to bring her mouth to his neck, to let her lips explore the skin against his nape.

Hannah leaned around his shoulder to see where they were headed. She didn't recognize the country road he'd taken, and she quickly tightened her grip on his waist as the motorcycle bounced over the ruts like a ball bearing rolling across a washboard.

She occupied herself with looking to the side, catching the recently planted corn and soybeans, looking like a sprinkle of green stubble in the fields that flashed past.

She knew that John was a farmer and Jake a carpenter, but she couldn't picture Jordan doing either of those things despite his apparent skill in building Esther's house. *This* was exactly how she could picture him, seated on a motorcycle like some highway god, fields flashing past him in a blur. He was raw sexual energy, his presence as potent and unsettling as the wind before a storm.

The motorcycle slowed to climb an incline, affording Hannah a view of the Mississippi River off to one side. It rolled somnolently under the rapidly darkening sky, small whitecaps flecking the surface as the wind gusted.

The motorcycle abruptly stopped, pressing Hannah hard against Jordan's back. He cut the motor and toed the kickstand into place.

"So what do you think?" he asked as Hannah climbed off and stood looking around, her back to him. Slowly she removed her helmet. Jordan was still sitting on the motorcycle, and she could feel him looking at her.

"This is beautiful," she said, admiring the rustic simplicity of the wood cabin. Dogwood and redbud trees bloomed in a riot of pinks, reds and whites above a carpet of green and purple. She couldn't immediately identify the wildflowers, but she had seen them often, growing beside the road. "Who owns this?" she asked.

"My brother Jake. It was Dad's old fishing cabin. Jake and John have done some work fixing it up. Jake's wife, Laura, planted the trees and flowers."

"She has a knack for landscaping," Hannah said.

"She likes flowers," Jordan said. "Like you."

He fell silent, and Hannah put up a hand to shield her eyes as the wind kicked up dust. The temperature was dropping rapidly as the storm moved in, and she shivered involuntarily.

"Come here," he said quietly from behind her, his voice low and commanding. The sound of it skittered up her spine, making her shiver again.

Slowly she turned and found him watching her, his eyes as fiercely blue as she'd ever seen them. He had hung his helmet on the handlebar, and now the wind played across his dark hair.

It was as if the wind pushed her toward him, and she took one step, then another.

Jordan's hands closed on her waist, and he lifted her, making her cry out in surprise. The next thing she knew she was sitting sideways on his lap as he straddled the motorcycle, the wind blowing in increasing force around them. She had dropped her helmet, and it came to rest at his feet.

His hands were still at her waist, and his face was only inches from hers. She shifted slightly, and Jordan smoothed one hand down her thigh, dragging her even closer to his chest.

Hannah's breath caught in her throat at the expression on his face.

The wind blew in a fierce gust, and Jordan's hand lifted to brush away a strand of hair caught on Hannah's cheek. To her surprise, his hand was trembling.

"I missed you all week," he said, his voice rough. "I wanted to call, but I was afraid I wouldn't be able to stop myself from coming to see you."

"Why didn't you come see me?" she whispered, her voice barely audible above the wind.

"Because I didn't think I could keep from doing this."

His head bent suddenly, his mouth taking hers so quickly and hungrily that it stole her breath away. Hannah's arms immediately wound around his neck, and she kissed him back fervently, answering the sexual tension inside her that clamored for more.

Hannah's breasts were pressed against Jordan's chest, and the pressure tightened her nipples, made her long for his caress there as well. She couldn't remember ever being this needy for a man's touch—for *this* man's touch.

As if reading her thoughts, Jordan slid one hand over the front of her cotton knit top and stroked her breast through the fabric. Tremors raced across her skin like ripples on the river.

"Do you know how...innocent you look in pink?" he demanded, bringing his head back far enough to look into her face. "You're the only woman I know who can dress like a Sunday school teacher and make me want you every time you look at me with those big eyes."

Hannah laughed, though she hadn't thought she was dressed much like a Sunday school teacher in her jeans and pink pullover with two small white buttons at her throat.

"Every time I look at you," he said, his voice husky, "I want to take you somewhere and make love to you. And not slowly and leisurely, either. Am I scaring you, Hannah Brewster?"

"No," she said, her own voice tight with need. "I want you the same way."

The first big drops of rain fell, hitting their faces, but still neither moved. They were caught in a sudden awareness of what they wanted and how much they wanted it. Jordan wasn't playing games now, and neither was Hannah.

The rain fell harder, soaking them both quickly, but they moved from their trancelike stillness only when thunder cracked loudly overhead.

Jordan lifted Hannah, her arms still around his neck, and swung his leg over the motorcycle. Carrying her pressed tightly to his chest, he strode to the cabin.

Under the relative dryness of the porch, he lowered her to her feet and pressed an urgent kiss on her mouth and neck while he fumbled in his pocket for the key.

When the door was open, he walked backward, tugging her inside, his mouth moving over hers. Hannah groaned, her hands clenched against his chest. Her breasts were heavy with anticipated pleasure, and her heart beat fast and hard.

Coolness enveloped them.

Hannah's eyes hadn't adjusted to the dark of the cabin, but she could feel a hardwood floor beneath her shoes. She tripped once, on a throw rug, she thought, and came up short against Jordan's chest. His breathing was ragged, a counterpoint to her own. Her hand trembled as she gripped his arm for balance.

He stopped walking and touched her face lightly with his hand before turning to a wood stove she could make out on the far wall. She looked around, barely registering her surroundings, as Jordan pulled two chairs to the front of the stove.

Hannah hugged her arms to herself, shivering slightly in her wet clothes.

Jordan stood up and pushed back the red-checked gingham curtains at the window, and faint light flooded the room.

"Come here," he said softly, and Hannah went, drawn to him like the rain to the ground below. She felt as giddy as she had as a girl when she was on a roller coaster and it slowly topped a hill, then began a dizzying descent that left her heart in her throat. She was falling like that now, but it was through air thick with need and pleasure.

"Hannah," he whispered softly. "I want you so badly. But the decision is yours."

She swallowed hard, incredibly moved that he would still ask her when her own need was so obvious.

"Yes," she whispered back.

Jordan cupped her face when she answered, his strong fingers stroking back her short hair. His eyes burned with such intensity that she felt he could see her very soul.

His mouth seared hers, his hands holding her head steady. Heat raced through her veins at his touch, and the cool interior of the cabin gave way to the fire in her heart.

It had been like this when she was with him before, and yet, not nearly as overwhelming. She felt as if her need for him had grown exponentially with the years.

He'll leave you again, a nagging voice told her, but she didn't care. He could say he was leaving her as soon as they'd made love, and she would still go to bed with him. It was useless to pretend that she could turn him down.

"What are you thinking?" he murmured, his fingers undoing the buttons at her throat.

Hannah smiled sadly, thinking of the time when he would leave her life again.

"I'm thinking that I'm a very foolish woman, because I can't seem to say no to you."

"You're not foolish," he said. "And I'm glad you can't say no, because I can't, either, where you're concerned."

"And when this is over?" she whispered shakily, unable to stop herself from asking the question. *How long do I have? How long before someone else turns your head?*

"I have a feeling I'll still want you no matter how many times we make love," he said fiercely, pulling the pink top over her head. He laid it over a chair and continued to undress her, his eyes locked with hers.

He might want her, she thought in desperation, but he would never stay with her. She would savor what she had now, because she would have to endure the pain of his leaving when it came.

Sensation overrode any anxiety she was still suffering as he slid her jeans down her hips. Hannah kicked off her shoes, and Jordan smiled as he knelt to pull her socks slowly from her feet. She had to steady herself with one hand on his shoulder.

"Do you know," he asked teasingly, "that you're the only woman who ever wore socks when I was about to make love to her?"

That made her think again of the other women to come after her, and she sighed.

"I'm sure you've seen more panty hose over the bedposts than I've ever owned," she said tartly, and Jordan laughed.

"You never tried to impress me, Hannah," he said as he drew the sock softly over her instep. "Men find that quality very sexy."

"You could have fooled me," she said honestly. "I haven't known other men."

It was a difficult admission, and if she hadn't wanted him so much now she never would have made it. But that only gave her another worry. What if he had taken off, the last time, because she was a lousy lover?

"So if you think I've been taking lessons in your absence," she said with as much bravado as she could muster, "you're wrong. Same old me."

Jordan startled her by standing and quickly picking her up in his arms again, leaving her jeans pooled by the chair. She clung to his neck, realizing that he was carrying her to the oak four-poster bed in the alcove off the kitchen.

"You underrate yourself, Hannah," he said sharply, nuzzling her neck as he laid her on the thick quilt that covered the bed. "You don't pretend, and that's what makes you so incredible."

She felt anything but incredible. She felt needy and vulnerable and wanton. What *was* incredible was the fact that she felt no shame about any of her emotions.

Jordan's eyes met hers as he pulled a foil packet from the front pocket of his jeans and placed it on the bed. He stripped off his clothes quickly, rolling them into a bundle and tossing them halfway across the room to land haphazardly near her jeans. Hannah still wore her underwear, making her feel almost virginal in the skimpy bra and panties.

"Let me," he whispered hoarsely when she reached behind her back to unclasp her bra.

She jumped slightly when thunder crashed overhead. Jordan leaned forward and kissed her neck and shoulders, soothing her as his fingers worked to remove the last of her

clothing. The rain came down in earnest, the room darkening as it lashed the windows.

Hannah felt her heart beating in a thunderous counterpoint to the storm as Jordan tossed her bra to the floor and
lay down beside her. He began stroking her breasts with
his hands, his thumbs making her nipples harden in excitement.

She arched upward, and he pulled off her panties, his
mouth taking the place of his hands on her breasts. He
kissed and suckled one and then the other, making Hannah
gasp and moan.

Her hands clutched his shoulders and then slid down his
chest, the dark springy hair against her palms leaving her
even more sensitized. She heard Jordan's breath catch as
her hands skimmed his stomach and went lower, touching
and caressing until he gave a guttural groan of pleasure.

"I want to go slowly for you, Hannah," he murmured,
his breathing uneven as he moved her hands away from
him.

"I don't think I can stand it if you go slowly," she told
him honestly.

Jordan smiled and touched her cheek with his fingers.
"Then we won't."

She shivered when his fingers did their own delicious
exploration of her body. When he touched her between her
thighs, she couldn't keep from whimpering with need. Jordan smiled and parted her legs, kneeling between them.

He opened the packet and put on the condom, and she
helped, making him groan again.

Hannah reached for him, pulling him to her, against her,
into her. As he slid inside her, she arched again with the
incredible sensations.

"Did I hurt you?" he whispered, leaning back to look
into her face, and she realized she had cried out from the
pleasurable feel of him.

"No," she murmured, shaking her head. "It's so good."
Jordan smiled. "For me, too." He moved inside her

slowly and carefully, and she knew that he was trying to prolong her pleasure. But the delicious tension was almost more than she could bear.

Hannah rose to meet his movements, her hands drawing his head down for a deep kiss. Whispers, sighs and soft groans mingled as their mouths sated themselves on each other. Hannah couldn't remember this devouring hunger the last time he had made love to her. She had never felt this fire in the blood before, not even in her dreams.

"Jordan...please," she whispered, and with a deep groan he moved faster. Neither of them could control the rising tide that flooded their bodies with a pleasure so pure and intoxicating that they moved as one.

Lightning flashed outside, and in the split-second that the room was lit, Hannah arched and gasped.

"Hannah..." The sound of her name was a cry in his throat, and he wasn't even sure he'd uttered it out loud as his own body shuddered with release.

She murmured something indistinct as she turned in his arms, and Jordan studied her face. He had never known another woman who responded to him the way Hannah did, with no artifice. She didn't try to impress him or wheedle anything out of him. And when she made love with him, she gave him everything, no holding back.

Except for one thing.

He had expected her to tell him about Kevin after their lovemaking. But she had only smiled at him and shifted drowsily. And then she had fallen asleep with her head on his shoulder.

What an intriguing woman she was, he thought in wonder. None of the other women he'd known possessed her sassiness, her easy smile or her talent for irritating him. And he'd come to look forward to all three of those things.

And his son was another source of wonder. Jordan felt a new dimension to his life opening when he was with Kevin. He had never realized how much fun it could be to watch a child grow and learn. He saw something of himself in Kevin, but it was something he realized now was in all children, the fierce desire to be loved and to find a place in the world.

As the youngest of three boys, Jordan had struggled to find his place in the world. He had worn his brothers' cast-off clothing as a boy, had competed for a place in sports where one or the other brother had already shone, had worked to find talents that were uniquely his.

He saw that same searching in Kevin. And he identified with Kevin's need for a father. Jordan's father had been a solitary man, spending long absences from his family, either working in the fields he farmed or going off on his own. Jordan's brothers had coped with that absence in their own way, but Jordan himself never felt that he quite fit in. He keenly felt the differences between what life was like and what he would like it to be.

Jordan had overcome the sense of being poor. He had all the money he required now. He had access to any number of attractive women who were all too glad to be seen on his arm at a fancy restaurant or at any of the social functions to which he was regularly invited. But they left him feeling restless and bored.

He glanced again at Hannah sleeping by his side, her short hair in disarray around her face. It made him smile just to look at her, at the tilt of her lips, stubborn even in sleep.

It was just like her to be so determined to raise his son by herself, to not even tell him that he was a father.

And what would he do once she finally told him? He sighed heavily. He didn't really know. He wanted time with his son, but beyond that, he couldn't make any promises.

Hannah stirred and slowly opened her eyes. She glanced down at the quilt he had pulled over her and then lifted her eyes to his face.

"What time is it?" she asked drowsily.

He smiled. "Why? Do you have to catch a bus?"

Hannah's mouth curled up as she laughed softly. "Not on your life. I got here by motorcycle, and I'm leaving the same way." She sat up, clutching the quilt to her chest, and looked toward the window. "Is it still raining?"

"A little. Most of the storm passed." He traced a line down her cheek with his finger, then turned her face to his.

"Are you in a hurry to leave?" he asked.

Hannah studied his face. "Are you?" she asked.

"No," he said quietly. "Not now." He couldn't promise any more than that. He didn't know what he really wanted beyond this moment.

"I'm used to thinking ahead, you know," she told him. "I'm one of those people who make appointments with the dentist and the doctor a year ahead of time. I make a grocery list before I go to the store. I read all the reviews before I see a movie." She slanted him a sideways glance. "You're the kind of man who does everything on the spur of the moment. I bet you don't even read a map before you start out on a trip, much less go to the bank to get change for the toll booths."

Jordan had to smile at that. "I usually check the gas gauge," he offered.

"You probably think the Boy Scout motto is just a suggestion," she countered. Then she sighed. "Jordan, when you're ready to walk away, I'd like to ask you to give me a little advance warning this time. Don't just walk out the door, saying, 'See ya later,' then never come back."

His heart contracted.

"I won't do that," he told her. "You know, I didn't exactly walk away from you before. I was swimming in paperwork for a couple of weeks, and when it was done I tried to get in touch with you. But you were the one who'd left without any forwarding address."

"It seemed pointless at the time," she said. "I assumed you'd moved on. I wasn't very sophisticated at bedroom games. I guess I'm still not."

"I didn't make love to you because of your innocence,"

he shot back, grasping the implication and wanting to convince her that she was wrong. "You aren't some bedspring challenge for me, Hannah! You never were. I made love to you because I liked what I saw when I looked at you. You made me laugh, and you exasperated me. And with you I felt more alive than I ever had."

He touched her arm, his fingers tightening around her wrist when she tried to pull away.

"Don't!" she said sharply. "I don't want to hear how much you cared for me, Jordan. Because I just don't believe it."

"Then believe this," he said tightly, dragging her toward him and tangling his other hand in her hair. "Believe what you feel when I do this to you."

His mouth took hers fiercely. She refused to respond at first, angry more with herself than him, because she wanted to believe him, wanted to believe that he had cared something for her and possibly still did. But her own body wouldn't let her remain passive in the face of his touch. A moment later she gave a deep moan of surrender and curled her arms around his neck.

Jordan urged her onto her back, then caressed her body from her throat to her breasts to her legs, making her writhe as her need for him quickly mounted. His mouth followed his hand, making her gasp when he touched her intimately, his thumbs stroking her inner thighs, his lips bringing fire to her inner core. She thought she would die with the pleasure of his ministrations.

Hannah couldn't form the words to tell him that she needed him inside her now. Her mouth opened, but only a hoarse whimper emerged.

But Jordan was as needy as she was. He moved over her and entered her quickly and without any preliminaries.

"Believe this, Hannah," he whispered, his voice raspy with desire. "If nothing else, believe this." And then he, too, was lost in the rising tide of overpowering sensations.

He said her name over and over as the pleasure exploded in them, for the moment wiping away both past and future.

They said nothing afterward, and Jordan moved to her side, his breathing slowly returning to normal.

Hannah remained awake this time, but Jordan lay so quietly beside her with his eyes closed that she thought he was asleep. She turned her head to study him, feeling her heart swell just at the sight of his strong body, the fine, hard muscles evident even as he lay relaxed.

She could spend a lifetime with a man as intelligent and gentle as Jordan. A lifetime, if he loved her. Her pulse leapt as she recognized the truth she had been hiding from herself. She was already in love with him.

She had tried to stop herself, but the futility of her efforts nearly made her laugh out loud in bitterness. She supposed that she was like dozens of other women who had fallen in love with Jordan McClennon. He never made promises; she had to give him that. The truth was evident all along, but she and those other women fell, anyway. They were as vulnerable as tin soldiers melting in a fire.

Well, St. Jude, let's see what you do about this.

The laugh died in her throat and came out a sigh instead. Jordan opened his eyes and turned his head.

"What's wrong?" he asked quietly.

"We should start back," she said, making a show of looking at the window. "The rain's stopped now. They'll all wonder where we are."

"I think they all have a pretty good idea where we are and probably what we're doing," he said dryly, and she flushed. "Don't do this, Hannah."

"Don't do what?"

"Don't pretend this meant nothing more to you than taking off your clothes to get a shower."

"I never have," she said sharply.

She slid off the bed, the quilt wrapped around her, and stooped to gather up her underwear. She dropped the quilt and quickly began dressing, aware that he was watching her.

"Then why are you doing this to us?" he asked impatiently.

"*Us?*" she demanded incredulously, pulling on her pink top that had dried over the chair. "You don't really expect me to believe there's an *us,* do you?"

Hannah knew he couldn't deny it. Furiously, she pulled on her jeans, still slightly damp, and sat on the chair to maneuver her socks and shoes.

"Why not?" he asked. "We're good together, Hannah. We make love like it's what we were born to do. Kevin likes me, and I enjoy spending time with him."

She stopped in the middle of tying her shoe and looked at him. "What are you saying?" she asked, her heart in her throat.

"I'm saying that I want to spend time with you and Kevin."

Spend time. The famous male phrase for getting into a woman's bed without benefit of commitment. It was almost funny how close those words were to *doing time,* which was no doubt how Jordan and other men of his ilk would describe marriage.

And the heartbreaking truth was that she didn't think she had the strength to deny him. Kevin would be crushed if he could never see Jordan again. And as for herself, in all honesty she had to admit that she wanted him in her bed even as she cursed her weakness for needing him. But she still had some pride.

"All right," she said, and he looked up suddenly from dressing. "You can spend time, as you put it. Spend time with Kevin and me. But I won't have you in my bed. I don't want my son growing up thinking that I compromised my principles for a few rolls in the hay."

Jordan studied her face until she lowered her head again to finish tying her laces.

"You can't deny you enjoyed this as much as I did," he challenged her.

"No, I can't," she said tightly. "And that's why I can't let it happen again. I'm a grown woman, Jordan, a woman with a son. And I'm not going to have him thinking that his mother lets herself be nothing more than some man's good time."

"You're a very tough woman, Hannah Brewster," he said softly.

"No, I'm not," she answered, then stood. "And that's why I hurt so much right now."

Hannah was glad they were on a motorcycle heading back to Esther's, because it prevented them from talking. Jordan had tried to comfort her before they left the cabin, but she wouldn't let him. For her own preservation, she had to keep her boundaries intact. He could never give her the commitment she wanted, and she could never tell him that she loved him.

She knew that he was angry with her when they got back on the motorcycle, but neither said anything more.

Hannah held her arms stiffly around Jordan's waist, trying to keep from thinking about the feel of his hard muscles beneath her hands. But her persistent memory of their love-making kept returning and she cataloged each detail and sensation for the cold nights when he would be gone from her life.

She knew with absolute certainty that he would be gone soon, because she was sure that Jordan McClennon would not be content with "spending time" with her and Kevin when he couldn't sleep with Hannah.

The sun was sinking behind raspberry-tinted clouds when the motorcycle turned into Esther's drive. Hannah took a deep breath, bracing herself for amused glances and teasing jokes.

But no one was in the yard when the motorcycle rolled to a stop, and she realized that it must be dinnertime.

Kevin threw open the door from inside the trailer and leaned out in excitement. "Hey, you guys!" he called. "What took you so long?"

Hannah felt herself flushing, but before she could answer Esther's hand reached out the door and tugged Kevin back inside. Then Esther leaned out and raised her brows.

"About time you got here," she said. She gave Hannah a hard, assessing look. "Did you eat the chicken?"

Hannah looked at her blankly before it occurred to her that the chicken was still stowed in Jordan's motorcycle.

"We got caught in the storm," Jordan said smoothly. "I'm afraid we had to abandon the chicken."

Esther eyed him skeptically. "Guess you were too busy." She held the door open for Jordan and Hannah as they stepped into the trailer.

Ronnie, Jake and John were crowded around the small kitchen table, eating hamburgers and fries. They all looked up as Jordan and Hannah came in, then quickly ducked their heads back to their food. Only Kevin, who had joined the men at the table, looked at them expectantly.

"So, did you find the drill?" Kevin asked, and a fit of coughing erupted around the table.

Hannah flushed, but Esther stepped forward to take charge. "I'm telling you McClennon boys to behave. You too, Ronnie. Eat your dinner, or there won't be any dessert. Hannah, you sit down here and help yourself. Jordan, there's beer in the refrigerator, if you want one."

Hannah self-consciously pulled out a chair, trying not to look at Jake and John on either side of her. She was uncomfortable not only because Jordan's brothers obviously knew what she and Jordan had been up to, but also because Jordan hadn't said one word to her since they left the cabin. She knew he was still angry with her after their argument, but the anger seemed to run far deeper than she'd first thought.

Jordan made no attempt to sit beside her, but moved to a chair between Ronnie and Kevin, elbowing Kevin teasingly and asking how he was handling his hamburger with that missing tooth.

Kevin grinned, basking shyly in Jordan's attention. Hannah sighed as she watched them. Her son was obviously attached to Jordan, and it was going to be very painful for him when Jordan went away. She could have ensured that Jordan would hang around at least a little longer by continuing to sleep with him, but she wouldn't do that. It was better that her son learn to handle loss now rather than watch his mother sell her principles to keep a man in their lives.

"I'd better go," Jake said, standing and stretching. "Molly's staying at a friend's house tonight, so Laura and I are going to take in a movie."

"Yeah, I got to get going too," John said as he scraped back his chair. "I told Rachel I'd come back home tonight. We're going out for a late dinner."

"More than dinner, I'd say," Esther mumbled, glancing at her watch.

John abruptly grinned and planted a big kiss on her cheek.

"Be happy, Esther," he teased her. "Two McClennon brothers are married off. And you've rattled the cage of the third one."

"I still got my work cut out for me," Esther complained, her eyes fixed on Hannah.

"We'll see you in the morning," Jake told her, giving her a hug before he and John left.

"You boys are going to be the death of me and St. Jude," she insisted, still scowling as the door closed on the two older McClennon brothers.

Ronnie dumped his paper plate into the trash and hurried toward the door, kissing his mother on the way.

"Gotta go," he said. "Movie."

"I think he's got a girl," Esther mused. "And he don't want me finding out."

"I wonder why," Jordan said dryly.

Esther's response was a grunt and a playful smack to the back of Jordan's head. He ducked and grinned at Kevin.

"Hey, Jordan!" Kevin said enthusiastically. "There's a Chuck Norris movie on TV. Wanna watch it with me?"

"Sure thing," Jordan said, evading Hannah's eyes as he stood, pushing the last of his hamburger into his mouth. She froze as he moved past her chair, but although it was a tight squeeze, Jordan was careful not to touch her. Ironically, she found his unwillingness to make physical contact more depressing than the fact that he was angry with her. If there was one thing they had going between them, it was physical attraction. Now, maybe she had killed that as well.

"So, do you want to talk?" Esther asked abruptly, and Hannah's head came up in surprise.

"Do I look like I want to talk?" she asked sadly, then immediately regretted her words. Summoning a smile, she patted the seat next to her.

"Talk, schmalk," Esther said, shrugging as she sat. "You look like a woman who's feeling sorry for herself. Want to trade war stories about lovers?"

Hannah colored, still embarrassed that everyone knew what she and Jordan had been doing at the cabin.

"Now don't go getting coy on me," Esther warned as she stood and rummaged in a cabinet above the refrigerator. She sat back down with a bottle of sloe gin in her hand and a glint in her eye.

"To men," Esther said, uncapping the bottle and pouring a generous amount into Hannah's glass of cola, then doing the same with her own glass. She held up her glass and clinked it with Hannah's. "They're messy suckers," Esther said, adding, "But, God love 'em, they're a fountain of youth in boxer shorts. Keep us from getting old too fast."

"I don't feel very young right now," Hannah offered, taking a long swallow and deciding she liked the taste, which reminded her of cherry cough syrup.

"That's because you're thinking with your head instead of your heart," Esther informed her. "When I first met the late Mr. Wardlow, God rest his soul, I said to myself, 'Esther, there's one fine man. But he could keep a girl from having the career she wants.' I wanted to be an actress in those days," Esther confided, leaning over and patting Hannah's arm. "And I told Mr. Wardlow as much. I almost didn't marry him, I was so full of my own plans."

"What happened?" Hannah asked, intrigued despite herself.

"Well, he said we would give my career a shot, and we went to California together after we got married. And nothing much came of it. I got tired of knocking on doors that wouldn't open, so we came back here. Raised some corn and beans and had Ronnie along the way."

"He made you happy," Hannah said, making it a statement more than a question.

Esther's eyes were dreamy. "Oh, yes, but I didn't even know it for a while. It was after Ronnie was two and we had a little girl. Pretty little thing, but she was born too early and she died." Esther sighed. "I couldn't eat or sleep for weeks after. I was wasting away in my grief. I was even thinking that I shoulda never married my husband, shoulda just gone out to California on my own and stayed. And then Mr. Wardlow came to me one night when I was sitting in the rocker just crying real quietlike. And he got down on his knees in front of me, and I could see he was crying, too. 'Esther,' he said, 'I miss our little girl, too. But I can go on if I got you. And right now I don't got you.'" Esther took a deep breath. "Well, right then and there I knew what a fool I'd been not to appreciate my Thomas Wardlow. He knew two people can get through most anything if they got each other. And he was right."

Hannah felt tears welling in her own eyes. "You must have loved each other a great deal."

"Oh, we did," Esther said. "And right then and there I dried my eyes and took him into my arms and told him so. And he was right. We got through whatever came our way all right from then on." Esther poured another helping of sloe gin into Hannah's glass. "It's all in getting what you need, not what you think you want, honey," Esther told her, winking. "Now, you up for a hot game of gin rummy?"

It was almost ten p.m. when Hannah tried to focus her eyes on the kitchen clock. "I'd better tell Kevin to get ready for bed," she said, hiccupping as she stood and quickly gripping the table as the clock swayed where it sat on the wall. "Oh, my," she said weakly.

"You got a little buzz on," Esther told her. "Why don't you go to bed and let Jordan handle Kevin? I heard him announce bedtime a half hour ago."

"He did?" Hannah asked, wide-eyed. "I didn't hear anything."

"That's because you was too busy tending your winnings," Esther said, shaking her head ruefully. "You're one lucky girl when it comes to gin rummy."

Hannah grabbed two of the vanilla wafer cookies from the pile on the table, her "winnings," and started toward the back bedroom. "Lucky in cookies, unlucky in love," she crooned, feeling incredibly giddy. "Good night, Esther."

Esther watched her with baleful eyes. "Good night, Hannah. Think I'll turn in myself."

Hannah made her way unsteadily through the darkened living room and toward the bedroom where Kevin was sleeping. The door was slightly ajar, the soft glow of a nightlight outlining the doorjamb. She stopped when she heard Kevin's voice.

"Should I put my tooth under my pillow, Jordan?"

"Why don't you put it here on the night table beside Esther's troll doll?" Jordan suggested.

"Okay. You won't forget to take me on your motorcycle tomorrow, will you?"

"No, I won't forget," Jordan said. "Now close your eyes."

"Sweet sleep," Kevin responded, picking up the next line of the good-night rhyme he always recited with his mother.

Hannah started to push open the door, thinking that Jordan wouldn't know the next line.

"Dream a dream," Jordan said, and Hannah stopped in surprise.

"For me to keep," Kevin finished.

"See you tomorrow, kiddo," Jordan said, and Hannah stood where she was, even though she heard his footsteps heading for the door.

"'Night, Jordan," Kevin called.

Jordan didn't seem surprised to see Hannah when he opened the door. He very calmly closed the door and started to walk around her.

But Hannah grabbed his arm just as a hiccup escaped her, and Jordan faced her, frowning.

"Have you been drinking?" he demanded.

"How did you know about the 'Close your eyes' thing I do with Kevin?"

"He told me," he said, still frowning and coming closer now to study her face in the dark. "You *have* been drinking, haven't you?"

"Just a little sloe gin," she said, letting go of his arm and turning away from him. She nearly lost her balance and reached out a hand for some support to clutch.

Just as suddenly, Jordan's hands were on her shoulders, propelling her toward the trailer door. Dazed and looking around for an ally to rescue her from Jordan, Hannah noted that only the light from a television glowed under Esther's closed bedroom door. So much for an ally, not that Esther would have been inclined to rescue her, anyway.

The warm night air enveloped her as soon as the front door opened, making her slightly dizzy. But when she balked, Jordan simply picked her up in his arms and carried her outside. He managed to turn around and pull the door closed before sitting down on the cement block step with her on his lap.

"What are you doing?" Hannah demanded, trying to get up but finding that the effort made her head spin again.

"Sobering you up," Jordan said. His expression looked irritated, but she thought she heard a note of amusement in his voice.

"I *am* sober," she said indignantly. "I'm just a little too warm, that's all."

"Oh, really?" Jordan said dryly, and the next thing she knew he was standing and carrying her toward the site of the new house. She clutched at his neck for balance, looking up briefly and wondering why the stars were moving so quickly.

"What are you doing?" she asked for the second time. "I'm perfectly capable of walking anywhere I want."

"Honey, you couldn't even *find* anywhere right now if you had a compass and a guidebook filled with maps."

He abruptly stopped walking and set her down on the ground on her bottom. She started to get up, but sank back with a groan as her head spun. When she glanced up at Jordan, he was holding a garden hose.

"What are you doing?" she asked, slightly alarmed by the dangerous look on his face.

"Is that the only thing you can ask?" he said mildly. "You said you were too warm, so I think I'll cool you off."

"No, Jordan!" she cried, putting up a hand in defense. "No, don't!"

"But, sweetheart," he teased her, "if you're as sober as you swear you are, just get up and walk away."

Hannah had to admit that moving was an impossibility at the moment, and she realized that he had the upper hand.

"All right, all right," she said. "I'm not sober. I had too much sloe gin. Oh, Lord, I think my head's going to come off." Near tears, she rested her head on her knees and groaned.

"Not tonight," he said cheerfully. "But I wouldn't bet on tomorrow morning."

He sat down behind her and gently tugged her back against his chest. Cool fingers softly massaged her forehead until she relaxed enough to rest her weight against him.

"It didn't *taste* like liquor," she moaned.

"I know. But, believe me, it has a kick."

"Oh," she moaned again. "I still can't find my locket. And I didn't tuck Kevin in. I didn't even tell him goodnight. Nothing's going right. This is awful. I'm his mother, and I'm drunk."

"You're entitled now and then," he said, sounding as if he were smiling again. "And I tucked him in."

"But you don't understand," she groaned. "The tooth fairy has to come, even if he doesn't believe. I can't let him down. You weren't there when he had the colic or cut his first tooth or said his first word. *I* was."

"It's all right," he said soothingly. "I'm here now. Kevin will be fine."

Gradually her panic subsided, and she surrendered to Jordan's quieting touch. When she gave a soft sigh on the edge of sleep, he carefully picked her up again and carried her back into the trailer. Temporarily putting her in the armchair, Jordan set up the sofa bed and turned down the sheets. He sat Hannah on the edge and held out his hand.

"Are you wearing contacts?" he asked.

Hannah blinked once and mumbled, "I think so."

"Put them in my hand, Hannah," he said. "Come on, honey."

Sighing with the effort it took, she held her head over his hand and popped out first one lens and then the other. Groaning, she toppled backward and was almost asleep in seconds.

She briefly awoke when Jordan sat her up to swallow a couple of aspirin, then sank back into sleep as a cool, damp washcloth was placed over her forehead. She thought she felt his lips on her cheek, but she was too tired to do anything more than sigh.

Jordan stood watching her in the dark for a long while, a somber expression on his face. She had come as close as she ever had tonight to admitting that Kevin was his son. A little more time, and he'd get the admission from her.

Maybe he hadn't been there for the boy in the past, but he was here now.

Gently he removed the washcloth from Hannah's forehead as she murmured incoherently in sleep. He traced his finger down her cheek and smiled softly as he thought about how hard she was struggling to keep him out of her life.

"You're losing this fight, Hannah Brewster, and that's a promise," he whispered.

But the fact that he had the upper hand now gave him little satisfaction. Instead he felt a strong urge to lie down beside her and take her in his arms.

And if he hadn't had to go play tooth fairy for his son, he might have done just that.

Eight

Hannah woke the next morning with a dry mouth, pounding head and queasy stomach. She tried to sit up and groaned as her head hurt even more. From outside she could hear the sounds of carpentry, and she felt as if the hammers and saws were working inside her head and stomach.

Esther peered around the partition from the kitchen.

"You still alive?" she wondered wryly.

"Yes, and I wish I were dead," Hannah moaned. "What hit me?"

"A bottle of sloe gin," Esther informed her, shaking her head. "You were pouring it in your glass like you was a sinner, and it was holy water. It has a bite, you know."

"Why didn't you tell me that last night?"

"Because you needed to unwind, and if it took sloe gin, then so be it. You're unwound, ain't you?"

"I'm so unwound that I may not survive," Hannah assured her. She tried to get off the bed and sank down again, clutching her head.

"You just stay put," Esther told her. "I'll bring you some aspirin. You got nothin' you got to do today. The boys are out working on the house, and Jordan took Kevin for a ride on his motorcycle." Esther chuckled. "The tooth fairy done left him a whole dollar, and he can't wait to spend it."

When Esther returned with the aspirin, Hannah was sitting on the edge of the bed, feeling morose and embarrassed.

"I'll never live this down," she said, swallowing the aspirin with the juice Esther handed her. "Everyone must be laughing at me."

Esther shook her head. "Don't you worry. Jordan told everyone that you have a sinus headache from the rain yesterday. He told them to leave you alone and give you some peace and quiet."

"He did?" Hannah said, not quite believing that Jordan would do that for her, especially after he had threatened to drench her with the hose the night before. It was one of the few things her sloe-gin-sogged brain remembered.

"That he did," Esther confirmed. "And when I went to Kevin's room to play tooth fairy last night, Jordan had already been there. You know, he's awfully good with that boy of yours."

"I know," Hannah sighed.

"And you've been pretty darned hard on him."

"I can't help it, Esther," Hannah said.

"And what did you do to him last night?" Esther demanded. "Or don't you remember since you were a wee bit, shall we say, tipsy at the time?"

"How do you know I did *anything* to him?" Hannah said.

"Because I saw his face this morning, Hannah Brewster. I may not know too much about books or the right way to talk and all that stuff, but I do know faces. And that man had a sadness in his eyes that hurt me to see.''

Hannah sighed and closed her eyes.

"It wasn't last night. It was yesterday when we were in Jake's cabin.'' She opened one eye to find Esther listening avidly. "And don't look at me like that,'' Hannah said. "I'm not about to tell you any details of what we did in the cabin.''

Esther held up her hand and sniffed indignantly.

"I certainly wouldn't pry.''

"Right,'' Hannah said wryly. Catching Esther's crestfallen expression she said, "I was hoping he'd tell me that he cared for me. Something like that,'' she added lamely. "But he didn't, and I told him that he could continue to see Kevin, but there would be no more…intimacy between him and me.''

Esther rolled her eyes. "And did you at least tell him that you love him?''

Hannah looked at her in surprise. "What makes you think I love him?''

"Think, schmink,'' Esther said, grinning. "St. Jude and me, we got our ways. Now you listen to me, Hannah. That boy may be a bit nervous about walking down the aisle, but he sure as heck ain't going to get over his shyness if you don't tell him what he needs to hear.''

"His shyness?'' Hannah blurted out, totally undone by Esther's assessment of Jordan. "I don't think we're talking about the same man here, Esther.''

Esther stood as they both heard the motorcycle pull into the drive.

"If I was you,'' Esther said, "I'd pretty up a bit.''

Hannah realized with dismay that she had slept in yesterday's clothes, her hair was tangled, and she had no recollection of washing her face. Groaning as she stood, she hurried to the bathroom.

Oh, my Lord, she thought in dismay as she surveyed her reflection in the bathroom mirror. Then a new worry hit her, and she leaned close to the mirror to look in her eyes. Her contacts. Had they fallen out in the bed?

But, no. There they were in their storage case on the sink, though she was positive she hadn't put them there.

Hannah could hear Kevin's excited voice as he came through the door, and she hurried to make herself presentable.

"Mom!" he was calling. "I gotta tell you about this!"

"Coming!" she called back, wincing with the loudness. "In a minute!"

When she left the bathroom ten minutes later, she had taken a quick sponge bath and brushed her hair. With a clean T-shirt on and her contacts in place, she almost felt like a new woman.

Until she saw Jordan leaning back against the kitchen counter. Then her heart began pounding and her stomach tied itself into knots again, and she was the same woman she was yesterday, still in love with a man who steered clear of any commitment.

"Mom!" Kevin cried, running to her and dragging her to the kitchen by the hand. "Mom, Jordan's motorcycle is *so* great! It's a Harley Bad Boy. Did you see how great it is?"

"A Harley Bad Boy," she repeated, looking at Jordan and then quickly looking away. He was smiling indulgently, but she could see the challenge in his eyes. He was daring her to make some comment about the name. "It's a very pretty bike, Kevin."

"Pretty?" Kevin cried in outrage. "Mom, you can't call something tough like that pretty! Oh, man."

Her son was so upset by her choice of words that Hannah had to laugh. But that made her head hurt, and she immediately winced. The movement didn't go undetected by Jordan.

"I have an idea," Jordan said to Kevin. "Let's take your mom somewhere quiet for a cup of coffee."

"Coffee," Kevin said with distaste. "Yuck. How about another milkshake instead?"

Esther cleared her throat. "I've got to get to the diner, Kevin. Why don't you come with me?"

"Hey, great," Kevin said. "It's okay, isn't it, Mom?"

Hannah gave her consent, still not looking at Jordan. She was feeling more than a little foolish today, and it didn't help that she couldn't recall exactly how she had gotten to bed the night before.

Esther gave Hannah a wink as she left with Kevin, and Hannah picked up her purse.

"We're not taking the Bad Boy, are we?" she asked lightly.

Instead of answering, Jordan put his hands on her shoulders and gently turned her to face him. The expression in her eyes was so soft and vulnerable that he wanted to wrap her in his arms and kiss away her worry.

But she would never let him do that. Not Hannah with her forthright, ironclad principles.

"I really should stay here and help with the building," she said, her voice tentative.

"You're in no condition to get near power tools," he said, his voice leaving no room for argument. "Come on."

He opened the door and she stepped out into the sun, blinking hard and feeling her headache surge into greater throbbing awareness.

"Hey, Hannah," Ronnie called as he stopped hammering. "How you feeling?"

"Better, thanks," she said, trying to smile as both Jake and John glanced up and waved.

Esther was right, she thought in relief. Jordan hadn't told anyone about last night.

Jordan watched her face as he helped her into the cab of John's truck. He was trying not to smile, but she was so damned embarrassed about getting drunk last night that it was all he could do not to tease her.

He had thoroughly enjoyed taking Kevin for a ride today,

but he hadn't been able to stop thinking about Hannah and wondering if she was all right. She had been so distressed about not tucking in Kevin. She had been the one who had seen her son through all the milestones of childhood. *You weren't there.* When she'd said that, his heart had nearly stopped. He had expected her to come right out with the rest of the words then. *You're Kevin's father.* But she hadn't.

But she was going to tell him. Jordan knew that she had to, sooner or later. And even though it was beginning to look like later, he was going to be there when she finally said the words.

Hannah didn't ask where they were going. It was enough to get away from the hammering and to let the clean morning air flow over her face from the open window. She was beginning to feel better already.

Esther's words kept recurring in her head. *And did you at least tell him that you love him?*

Those were the last words that a man like Jordan wanted to hear. He and his Harley Bad Boy would disappear into thin air like dust on a windy day. And she'd never feel his arms around her again. Hannah had the feeling that when Jordan left this time, she would never see him again. It was such a sorrowful thought that she sighed.

"Do you feel sick?" Jordan asked.

Hannah shook her head. "I don't wish I were dead now, if that's what you mean."

Jordan smiled. "Coffee will help. And some peace and quiet."

Quiet, maybe. But Hannah didn't think she was going to have any peace in her heart for a long time.

Jordan stopped at a fast-food drive-through and ordered two coffees and a Danish. Hannah didn't ask where they were going, but she noticed that he was taking the river road.

He pulled the truck over where the river made a bend, leaving a lush expanse of grass complete with picnic table and plenty of shade. In summer there was almost always a family enjoying a leisurely lunch at the spot.

"Come on," he said. "The doctor prescribes fresh air with your coffee."

He helped her down from the truck and led her to the picnic table, seating her on the bench so that she faced the river with her back to the table. Jordan sat down beside her.

Off to their right, Hannah could see an older man slowly and laboriously picking wildflowers and putting them into a jar of water.

Hannah sipped her coffee, closed her eyes and tilted her head back to let the breeze trail over her face. They sat in silence for several minutes, and Hannah was beginning to relax.

"Jake's wife, Laura, is pregnant," Jordan said quietly. "The baby's due at Christmas."

Hannah opened her eyes and looked at him. He was still staring out at the river, but there was a restlessness to his features that made her think of a man about to say goodbye.

"Jake must be very happy," she said noncommittally.

"Oh, he is," Jordan said. "I've never seen him like this before, so…content. He's a man who was meant to be married. Laura is the best thing that could have happened to him."

"'One man's meat is another man's poison,'" she quoted dryly.

"I've never been able to settle down with one woman," Jordan said quietly. "I suppose it just isn't in me. Three weeks, one month, tops, and I need to move on."

Hannah swallowed, realizing that her month was almost over.

"Is that what you really want?" Jordan asked. "Spending the rest of your life with the same man, waking up beside him every morning, watching him gradually gain weight, lose his hair and his hearing? I've never understood what's so romantic about that kind of life, the same boring thing over and over.''

"Marriage is so much more than that," Hannah said, surprising herself with the passion in her voice. "To you, marriage is like the hand-me-down clothes you wore as a kid. They were used, and they represented something you didn't like—being poor.

"Marriage makes you rich in all the ways that count. No one stays young and undimmed forever. But a marriage partner always carries that ideal image of their mate in their heart. They've seen them at their best and at their worst, and they stay because that person is as dear and as necessary to them as the air they breathe.''

"How did you know that?" he asked, surprised. "About the hand-me-down clothes.''

"You talked a little about your early life when we went out to dinner. That first time.''

It amazed him that she had remembered. He supposed he had been making conversation at the time, though it was unlike him to confide something like that on a first date. Hannah's smile could make him do strange things.

"So why haven't you married, Hannah?" he asked softly, making her fidget under his penetrating gaze.

"I guess I haven't...found what I want," she said haltingly, the words she wanted to say crowding into her throat and nearly making her gasp for breath.

"What is it you want?" Jordan asked.

"Hello!" called the man picking flowers, and Hannah gratefully turned to look at him. He was even with them now, and she could see that he was slightly stooped and moving slowly, probably because of arthritis. "A beautiful day, isn't it?" he said happily.

"That it is," Jordan agreed as the man moved closer to them, bending down to pluck wild violets along the way. "Who are the flowers for?"

"My wife," the man said, straightening and smiling. "She had hip replacement surgery, and she can't get around too well yet. We always come up here by the river for a picnic in the spring and the fall. She's a flower nut,'' he said, laughing. ''Got so many flower beds our house looks like that Shaw's Gardens down in St. Louis. But I don't mind. She was so disappointed that she'd be missing the spring violets. 'How can you miss those when you got so much other stuff at home?' I asked her. And she said that a person should never get tired of looking at flowers.'' He chuckled again. ''These are going to make her so happy.''

They talked with the man a few more minutes about his wife's surgery, and then he moved on slowly, gathering violets as he went.

''Can you eat something now?'' Jordan asked Hannah after a few moments of companionable silence. He nudged the Danish toward her.

''Thanks,'' she said. ''I'm feeling a lot better after the coffee.''

When they finally stood to leave, Hannah looked back down the river where the old man had almost filled his jar with flowers. She felt something sad and wistful inside.

''Jordan,'' she said, stopping him with a hand on his arm. She nodded toward the old man. ''*That's* what I want. Someone who will do that for me when I'm old.''

He looked at the old man briefly, then slowly shook his head and started back to the truck.

Hannah's heart was heavy as she followed.

It was raining in St. Louis Monday morning when Hannah got up, and the bleak day suited her mood. She got Kevin off to school and ran some errands before heading to work at noon. She was scheduled for the late shift, and she wasn't looking forward to locking up the library at eight-thirty that evening. She was still feeling worn out from the weekend when she turned her car into the library parking lot.

Jessie, the summer intern, was waiting at the circulation desk when Hannah walked in.

"Your man was here," she breathed, her blue eyes wide. Jessie was a college student torn between two majors, library science and theater. Hannah's personal opinion was that she belonged in the theater department.

"What man?" Hannah asked as she put her purse in the office.

"You know," Jessie said as if Hannah were being deliberately obtuse. "The man you're seeing."

Hannah immediately snapped to attention.

"Tall, black-haired hunk," Jessie said appreciatively. "Wearing really nice clothes. Italian suit, I'd say. The shoes looked Italian, too."

"Jessie," Hannah said, "have you ever thought of going into fashion instead of the theater?"

"Hey, there's an idea," Jessie said, brightening even more, if that was possible. "Maybe I could go into costuming and combine theater and fashion."

"Good idea. Did he say what he wanted?"

"Who?"

Hannah sighed. "The tall, dark man in the Italian suit."

"Oh, him. No, but he left you this." Jessie fished in the drawer where overdue book fines were kept and pulled out a folded note. "I bet he's got a six-pack for a stomach."

"A what?" Hannah asked, startled.

"A six-pack. That's what you call good stomach muscles, because when they're well developed, you can see six of them."

Hannah suddenly felt as if she had become a stranger in the land of youth. She didn't understand the jargon anymore. She slipped the note into the pocket of her beige linen slacks and waited until Jessie had headed for the stacks with a cart filled with books. Then she slipped into the office and pulled out the slip of paper. Taking a deep breath, she read.

She frowned and read again.

"When you get off work, come to my apartment. Kevin will be here."

What was going on? Kevin was supposed to be picked up at school by his baby-sitter. What would he be doing at Jordan's apartment? He had penned the apartment address at the bottom, almost as an afterthought. As if he supposed she might not remember where it was after so many years.

Hannah opened the phone book to find Jordan's office number, then closed it again. Why had he come here in person, then left such an enigmatic note?

She spent the afternoon in a prolonged state of distraction, catching herself forgetting to go get the videotapes that patrons wanted to check out, and leaving them with an empty box instead, scanning the same book twice with the computer wand and then forgetting to scan the patron's library card.

"The Italian suit's got you rattled, doesn't he?" Jessie asked, grinning, as Hannah turned a book around after trying to scan it upside down.

"Not rattled," Hannah said. "Just…curious."

"Yeah, I know a few things I'd be curious about if I had a chance with him," Jessie said, her grin widening.

To her dismay, Hannah felt herself blushing.

"Are you living with him?" Jessie asked casually, and Hannah dropped the three books she was carrying to the return cart, making an elderly couple look up from their browsing at the magazine racks.

"Living with him?" she repeated. "Where did you get that idea?"

"I was working on Saturday when Mrs. Peterson came in, and she asked how you and your live-in were doing."

"Mrs. Peterson needs to get a life," Hannah said darkly.

Jessie laughed. "Oh, she has a life all right. She's become quite the collector since her divorce. She tracks down and propositions every male over the age of eighteen who isn't married or tattooed. And, actually, I think she waives those two requirements from time to time. Do you know what she checked out?"

"No, but I bet you're going to tell me."

Jessie nodded, her eyes sparkling. "*How to Marry a Rich Man* and *Recipes for a Seduction*. She says she wants to learn how to fix oysters Rockefeller. They're an aphrodisiac, you know."

"So I've heard," Hannah said dryly.

"If I were you, I'd keep my eye on your Italian suit," Jessie chirped before she bounced away to tag the new magazines.

"He's not my Italian suit," Hannah called after Jessie.

The rest of the evening crawled as slowly as a snail on Valium. Hannah kept watching the clock, sure that the minute hand was stuck.

When she finally locked up at eight-thirty, she hurried to her car and drove away so quickly that Earl, the night watchman, teasingly jumped back from the curb as if she might run over him in her haste.

Jordan's apartment was downtown, and it took her fifteen minutes to get there. The doorman nodded to her, apparently expecting her. Impatiently she pushed the elevator button.

Hannah stepped out on Jordan's floor, absently taking in the plushly carpeted hall. She found his apartment and rang the bell. Seconds later he opened the door.

Hannah had prepared an entire speech to deliver. She wanted to know what Kevin was doing here, and she intended to tell Jordan that she hadn't appreciated the brevity of his note.

Her fine speech deserted her the moment she saw him.

He was wearing tight jeans, and his chest was bare. He had apparently just gotten out of the shower, because his hair was still wet. The blackness gleamed with a sheen of water.

Jessie was right, she thought in distraction. She could count six distinct muscles on his stomach.

"I thought I'd be long out of the shower before you got here," he said apologetically, standing back and holding open the door. "I showed Kevin around the health club.

We lifted some weights, and then I taught him how to play raquetball.''

"What's he doing here?" she asked without preamble.

Jordan shifted his shoulders. "Can I get you something to drink?"

"Jordan," she began, but he held up his hand.

"A drink first. I think you might need it."

"Oh, my Lord. Is he all right?"

"Yes, he's fine," he assured her quickly. "He just had a little trouble. Do you want some white wine? I don't have any sloe gin," he added dryly.

Hannah nodded, and Jordan walked to the bar against the far wall. Too anxious to sit down anywhere, Hannah looked around. The blue carpeting was so soft and thick that she felt as if she was sinking into it. The walls in the living room were covered on the upper half with a cream-colored wallpaper with a small, dark blue trefoil design. The bottom half of the wall was paneled with dark wood and topped with a chair rail. There were large windows on one side of the room. On two of them the thick blue curtains were pulled closed. The third was open and afforded a spectacular view of the Mississippi River and the landmark arch beside it.

She didn't remember this room very well and guessed that it had been redecorated since she'd been here before. Looking around some more, she recognized the built-in bookcases on either side of the stone fireplace. She thought of the do-it-yourself bookcase Jordan had given her, and suddenly she felt terribly out of place in the apartment.

When she turned around, Jordan was holding out a glass of wine to her. She thanked him, took a quick sip, then set it on the glass coffee table in front of the huge, sectional couch.

"Where's Kevin?" she asked, her voice sounding far more calm than she felt.

"He's getting his bath now," Jordan said.

"Why? He's not spending the night here."

"Hannah, I'm asking you to let him stay. Just for tonight. Both of you. I have two guest bedrooms, so you don't have to worry that Kevin will think you're compromising your principles." The last was spoken with a tinge of sarcasm, but she ignored it.

"I can't do this, Jordan. I just want to see my son."

"Hannah, please. Just sit down and let me tell you what happened." He put his hand on her arm, and she let him seat her on the couch. Again she felt as if she were sinking into luxurious softness.

He handed her her glass of wine again, and she took another sip.

"Kevin got into a fight at school," he said, his eyes fixed on her face.

"Kevin never fights," she said immediately.

"That's why he's so worried about what you'll say."

"My son can tell me anything," she protested.

"I know that," he said, holding up a hand to calm her. "But he knows how much you dislike fights of any kind, and he's worried that you'll be disappointed in him."

Hannah sighed, concern for her son overwhelming any irritation she felt toward Jordan.

"What was the fight about?" she asked.

Jordan's eyes left her face, and he frowned into his own glass, which she guessed held something stronger than her wine.

"It was a typical kid thing," he said evasively.

"Jordan, he's my son," she said. "I want to know."

He looked at her again, his eyes kind but determined.

"Some of the boys were teasing him about not having a father," he said, waiting for her reaction.

Hannah shook her head, unable to believe it. "Several of those kids are the product of divorce," she said. "Their fathers don't live with them, either."

"That's just it," Jordan said. "Their father may not live with them, but at least they know what the guy's name is. They were calling Kevin a bastard. He took a swing at one of them, and two more jumped him. He put up quite a fight, and luckily, at that age, kids can't hit hard enough to do a lot of damage. He's just got a couple of bruises. But he was so upset, that his teacher thought he ought to come home." Jordan paused. "He asked her to call me. I explained things to his sitter on the phone—more or less. Hannah, I'd really appreciate it if you'd forget that Kevin threw the first punch. He was…provoked."

Hannah lowered her head to her hands in dismay. How had it come to this with her son? Had he always wanted a father so much, and had she been so blind to that want?

"Hannah," Jordan said gently, "don't you think it's time to stop this charade?"

She barely heard him, so awash in guilt that she could only think of Kevin and what he must have gone through.

"I've got to talk to him," she said, standing.

"Hannah, wait—"

Before she could take more than two steps toward the hallway to her right, Kevin appeared in the doorway.

"Hi, Mom," he said tentatively.

Hannah couldn't move for a moment, taking in the small bruise on his cheek and the red, swollen bump on his forehead. He looked so worried and so tired. The next instant she was hurtling herself toward him, kneeling beside him and hugging him fiercely to her.

"Are you all right, honey?" she murmured into his hair, then held him away to get a better look.

"Yeah, sure, Mom," he said, but despite his casual assurance, there was genuine relief in his eyes. "I thought you'd be pretty mad at me. I never got sent home from school before."

"No, of course not," she said. "It wasn't all your fault." She wasn't going to say anything about the fact that he threw the first punch, not because Jordan had asked her not to, but because he was right. She would have punched those kids herself.

So this is what it had come to, she thought as she hugged

Kevin again. In an age of divorce and families ripped asunder, the one shameful thing was not to know who your father was.

"Tomorrow we'll talk about what we're going to do about this," she said, smiling as she leaned back to look at Kevin. "But tonight I think you need some rest. Are you hungry?"

Kevin shook his head. "Jordan got us hot dogs and beans for dinner and then some ice cream."

"I'd say you're pretty well fed then," she said, gently brushing her finger over his bruise. "Does your face hurt?"

He shook his head and grinned at her. "Jordan put some gunk on it, and he said he thought I was brave."

Hannah felt tears well in her eyes. "I think so, too."

"Mom, can we stay here tonight?" he pleaded. "There's more ice cream in the freezer."

"Are you trying to bribe me?" she teased, but she knew that she was relenting. She couldn't stand to see him hurt, and if spending the night here would make him feel better...

"Can we?" he insisted.

"All right," she said. "But just this once. Come on. Show me where you're sleeping. What do you say to Jordan?"

Kevin leaned around Hannah and grinned at Jordan. "You were right. She didn't get mad at all."

"That's not what I meant for you to tell him," she said, not succeeding at all in sounding stern.

"Thanks, Jordan," Kevin said. "Good night."

Jordan called good-night, but he didn't follow, and Hannah hesitantly trailed Kevin to the bedroom. It was large and as tastefully furnished as the living room. Kevin stripped to his Batman undershorts and crawled into bed.

Hannah sat on the edge of the bed, ostensibly to pull up the covers and pat his pillow.

"Kevin," she said gently, "about your wanting a father..."

"It's all right, Mom," he said around a yawn. "Jordan's going to be my dad. Wait'll the kids at school get a load of him. I bet he could turn their dads inside out."

"It's not a contest, you know," she reminded him, worried that when Jordan moved on to other things, Kevin would be left worse off than ever.

"Mom, I'm not trying to win," he told her earnestly. "But I got lucky. I couldn'ta found a better dad than Jordan."

Or a more unlikely one, Hannah thought. But she would keep her worries to herself, at least around Kevin. He had a right to his dreams. She was the one with no excuse for wanting the impossible.

When she came back into the living room, Jordan was sitting on the couch, holding his glass on his knee. He gave her a tight smile. He still hadn't put on a shirt, and she couldn't stop herself from nearly gawking at his bare chest.

"He fell asleep almost immediately," she said awkwardly. "It must have been a rough day for him."

"He's a good kid," Jordan said. "He'll get through this." He seemed about to say something else, then didn't. Instead, he held out his hand to her.

"You look so pretty tonight," he said.

Hannah took his hand and let him pull her down onto the couch next to him.

"You look...healthy," she finished haltingly, not finding an adequate description for the virile splendor that kept drawing her eyes to his chest. She wanted to touch him there, but she didn't dare. She knew that she wouldn't be able to stop.

Jordan laughed. "I don't think I've been called that before, except in a doctor's office."

"Jessie—the girl you gave the note to in the library—was quite impressed with you. And your suit," she added.

Jordan laughed again, but his eyes remained on Hannah's face. He looked so enticing that she swallowed hard.

"Sit back and relax, Hannah," he told her softly. "You

look like you're expecting me to pounce on you any minute.''

"And of course that never crossed your mind," she said primly, making his lips turn up at the corners in a mischievous grin. She looked away, pretending to study a painting on the opposite wall.

"Of course it crossed my mind," he told her. "Ravishing you crosses my mind about sixty times a day. But, believe it or not, I respect your *principles*."

He said the word as if he didn't believe that it was the true issue at all. Hannah frowned and looked back at him again.

"I have my son to think about," she said carefully.

"I know," he said impatiently. "And I understand." He smiled again, a smile that didn't quite reach his eyes. "But my libido doesn't grasp that particular principle."

Hannah sighed. "Maybe I should go."

Jordan shook his head. "No, it's all right. Here, drink your wine."

She took the glass from him and swallowed deeply. "So what are we going to do about this...problem of ours?" she asked boldly. Her eyes met his, and she felt herself drawn deeper, as if by some seaborne current.

Jordan studied her expression, his eyes darkening. He brought her hand to his naked chest where she felt his heartbeat, strong and fast. Her own began galloping in response, and her mouth felt suddenly dry.

Her hand was shaking, and she quickly set the wineglass back on the table.

"Did you ever do any necking as a teenager?" he asked, his voice soft and seductive.

Hannah shook her head. Trying to keep her sister in line had precluded much of a social life of her own.

"It goes something like this," he said, bringing his mouth to hers and kissing her lightly and teasingly. Hannah swallowed a groan and tried to deepen the contact.

"It's both arousing and frustrating," he continued, his

lips leaving hers to trail down the side of her neck. Hannah pressed closer to him, her own hand skimming over his chest.

Jordan's fingers played over her blue silk blouse, tantalizing her breasts until her nipples hardened with desire. Then he began to slowly unbutton her blouse.

At that, Hannah felt sanity return.

"Kevin's just down the hall," she whispered worriedly, drawing back from him.

But Jordan only smiled that lazy, seductive smile and continued stroking her with one hand.

With the other hand he reached out to a remote control on the table and held in a button. The lights dimmed, and when the room was almost dark he released the button. Then he got up and walked to the hallway where he pulled two sliding wooden doors together to close it off from the living room.

He came back to her and sat down, then pressed another button on the remote control.

"If Kevin leaves his room, that nightlight over the door will come on. There's another one in the hall, so he can find his way in the dark. If the light comes on, we'll have ample time before he gets to the doors."

Ample time for what? she wondered. To pretend they weren't engaged in anything more than small talk here in the dark?

"You have a lot of gadgets here," she said instead.

"I do run an electronics company, you know," he told her, and there was that smile again. "Now relax."

But that was easier said than done with his hands back on her blouse, unbuttoning it and driving her wild with delicious sensations. The blouse ended up on the couch, and her bra quickly followed. That made Hannah nervous again, even as it pulled her further into a whirlpool of need.

"We aren't..." she began, unsure of how to proceed.

Jordan shook his head. "No, we aren't. I told you. Just

some old-fashioned necking. Don't worry. You'll have plenty of time to get your clothes on if Kevin wakes up.''

Clothes on? That meant he was intending to undress her completely, and she felt her nerves sing with anticipation. No, she shouldn't be doing this. But even as she thought it, his mouth lowered to her breast and began a slow, gentle sucking.

She was sinking again, and a muffled whimper escaped her mouth before she could stop it. She tangled her hands in his dark hair, letting the silky strands sift through her fingers.

''Oh,'' she murmured softly, arching her back. ''Oh, Jordan.''

''Do you like this?'' he asked as he pulled back fractionally. In the dark she could still see the flame that never left his eyes. He was obviously satisfied with her response.

''Yes,'' she whispered. ''Yes, I like it very much.''

''Good. Because there's more to necking, you know. Much more.''

With that, he tugged her toward him and turned her until he could pull her onto his lap. Her legs were stretched out on the couch and her arms around his neck. His hard thighs were pressed against her legs. She felt wanton and incredibly aroused.

''Jordan, I—''

But he silenced her with another kiss, this one as teasing as the first, his mouth stroking hers softly, then pulling away and coming back again. His hands continued to stroke her breasts.

Hannah was breathing faster, and her hands moved down to caress his hard, broad shoulders, the muscles beneath her hands cording as she touched them.

Then his tongue was teasing her breasts again, and she moaned. His hand moved to her waistband, and she felt him unbuttoning her cream-colored slacks and sliding the zipper down. Then his fingers were stroking her stomach and upper thighs, trying to part her legs, making her moan again.

When he finally touched her where she was most sensitive, she felt an electric jolt course through her.

"Jordan," she gasped. "If you keep this up I'll... Let me touch you."

He hushed her with gentle kisses that moved their way to her ear. "It's all right," he whispered. "This is for you."

She had another moment of near panic when he said those words, but the heated thrumming of pleasure in her veins overrode the last of her doubts. She felt like a guilty teenager caught in the throes of passion, and to her amazement it was thrilling as well as incredibly arousing.

His mouth on her breasts and his fingers playing lower soon had her squirming and whimpering against him. She dropped her head to press her mouth against his shoulder, needing the contact with his bare flesh. Jordan took his cue from her breathing, matching the pace of his ministrations to her rising pleasure.

He could spend an eternity watching her expressive face, he thought, startling himself with the mental observation. But it was true. She didn't try to hide her pleasure, and the increasingly sensual movement of her hips was driving him crazy. But he had sworn to himself that he would honor her determination not to sleep with him again, and he meant it.

He knew that he was only increasing his own physical frustration by doing this, but he had never wanted to pleasure a woman so much before.

She was making soft noises, and he felt a surge of pleasure himself as he watched her. She was so soft, so vulnerable.

As tremors rippled through her, Hannah buried her face against his neck. The sound of her voice murmuring his name lingered sweetly with him as he gently stroked her hair and soothed her.

When she raised her head, her eyes were lustrous.

"Jordan," she said, unable to find words to tell him what she felt. He smiled and kissed her.

She felt his thighs shift beneath her, and she realized how one-sided the pleasure had been. He was obviously aroused and unsatisfied—and probably very uncomfortable.

"Let me," she began, reaching to touch him, but he caught her hand and brought it up to kiss it.

"Not tonight," he whispered. "Tonight was for you."

"Thank you," she murmured, feeling suddenly shy.

He held her a while longer, and she pressed her mouth against his bare chest, loving the taste and feel of him. She realized that she might have abandoned her high-minded declaration of principle tonight if he had asked, but he hadn't. He had taken care to give her pleasure instead, and she was left with a sense of wonder and an even deeper love for him.

Nine

Hannah had slept well in the huge, soft bed in the second guest bedroom. She didn't have to be at the library until noon again, so she had only to worry about getting Kevin to school on time. And he was more than cooperative now that his mother had taken the news of his fight so calmly.

Hannah peeked into the kitchen before she entered, bowled over again by the size and design of Jordan's apartment. The kitchen was large by her standards, anchored in the center by an island counter with a grill. Colorful tile in melon and sage tones ran riot everywhere.

Jordan was pulling a skillet from the stove when she sauntered in, wearing one of his shirts with the sleeves rolled up. He groaned when he saw her.

"How am I going to get to work with you looking like that?" he asked teasingly.

Hannah laughed. "I'm sure I'm a vision of temptation with no makeup and my hair looking like it slept in a blender."

"You are," he assured her. "I told you before—you undervalue yourself. Here, have some breakfast. I've got to get to the office early this morning."

She sniffed in the skillet's direction appreciatively. "What's that?"

"Fried potatoes, sausage and eggs." He pulled on his suit coat and stopped to press a kiss on her nose. "By the way," he said casually, "I'll see about getting you a key to the apartment."

"A key?" she said blankly.

"So you can get in whenever you want."

"Jordan, I don't think that's a good idea," she hedged.

"Why not? Is a key an infringement on your principles?"

"It's just that…" She didn't know how to put it. He was eroding her boundaries bit by bit, and she suspected that a simple key would lead to a lot more.

Jordan shrugged. "We'll talk about it later. Incidentally, I have to attend a dinner tomorrow night with some clients. Can you come?"

"What?"

"You don't have to dress up. I'll pick you up at six-thirty. Okay?"

He was already at the door while Hannah gaped at him.

"I guess so," she said, surprised by the sudden invitation.

"Great. I'll stop by your place tonight after you get off."

He left, and Hannah stood in the kitchen feeling that she had just lost another round to Jordan, though she wasn't sure why. They weren't waging war, she reminded herself.

Or were they? She was fighting with all of her inner strength not to give in to what Jordan wanted, a relationship that suited him but was devoid of commitment. He could come and go as he pleased until the day when he would go away forever.

* * *

Hannah paused to look at the pansies nodding in the glow from the streetlight before she opened the door to her apartment building. Jordan had taken root in her life as easily as the flowers had.

And he had made her aware of the many things she had missed in life, like "necking" with him the night before.

She unlocked her door and walked in to find Jordan sitting at her breakfast bar, a sheaf of papers spread out before him, his laptop computer screen glowing from its perch next to the papers. His tie was loosened and the first button of his dressy white shirt opened. She just stared, dry-mouthed, a moment before coming to her senses.

Jordan looked up and smiled at her as she closed the door firmly. She could smell popcorn.

"Hi, Mom!" Kevin called from the couch where he was conducting a mock battle with his superheroes. "My homework's all done, and Jordan and me read a book together."

"How was school today?" Hannah asked, ignoring Jordan for the moment and crossing the room to hug her son.

"Fine." Kevin shrugged. "I told everybody that my father is coming to the picnic Friday—on his motorcycle. Boy, that shut 'em up." He grinned at Hannah.

Hannah glanced over her shoulder at Jordan, but he was working on his computer again, staying out of her interchange with her son.

She wanted so badly to ask him why the baby-sitter wasn't here, but she didn't want Kevin to see how addled Jordan's presence made her. She ruffled his hair instead and gave him another hug.

"Are you ready for bed?" she asked.

"Yeah, I just gotta brush my teeth. Can't I stay up tonight, Mom? School's almost over."

"*Almost* doesn't cut the mustard," Hannah informed him, smiling nonetheless. "Go brush your teeth and I'll be in to say good-night."

"Mom?"

"What, honey?"

"Aren't you glad that Jordan's going to be my father? Because I'm really glad."

She glanced back over her shoulder again, noting that Jordan was openly watching her now, his eyes grave.

I'd be a lot happier if he put it in writing. But she didn't say that to her son whose happiness was nearly complete at this moment.

"I'm happy for you, Kevin. And that's what matters."

He accepted that, hugging her again, then headed toward the bathroom with a cheerful good-night to Jordan.

Hannah sighed, feeling tired and out of sorts.

"What did you do with the baby-sitter?" she demanded.

"I didn't toss her out the window, if that's what you're thinking," Jordan said, sounding a bit testy.

"Then where is she?"

Jordan took a deep breath. "I came over and sent her home early."

"And she went, just like that?" Hannah asked doubtfully. "Without any questions about just what you're doing here."

"You forget I talked to her yesterday after I brought Kevin home from school. Besides, she'd already heard all about me from Leslie at the grocery store," he informed her.

So that was it. The whole world was sanctioning—or at least publicizing—her relationship with Jordan, and he was taking shameless advantage. Even Kevin believed that Jordan was magic, that he was the father he'd wanted for so long.

"Giving a child what he wants is never easy," she said, deciding she might as well face Jordan now on that issue. "You should understand how vulnerable children are."

"Giving Kevin what he wants is easy," Jordan said, standing and making his way to the couch. "It's what you want that's difficult."

"And what do I want?" She forced herself to look into his eyes, struck as always by their intensity.

Jordan reached out to brush a strand of her hair from her cheek. His smile didn't reach his eyes.

"You want the impossible, Hannah."

"Why?" she demanded. "Why is it so impossible?"

"Just for me," he said. "It's not impossible for everyone."

"And what if it's not everyone I want?" she asked, coming as close as she ever had to telling him that she loved him. But she wouldn't say the words. Not when she was sure they would send him away from her.

He lifted his shoulders expressively. "You knew how it would be with me."

"And yet you pushed yourself into my life," she shot back. "Why, Jordan, when you knew you couldn't promise me or Kevin what we need?"

"Because—" He abruptly broke off the words. *Damn her!* She was trying to make him say what he should have told him a long time ago—that Kevin was his son, too. But he wasn't going to do it. He wanted her to tell him, and he would wait as long as it took.

Jordan still had his freedom to come and go, and he knew that it would change once the words were spoken, once she acknowledged that Kevin was his. When that happened, she would have the right to make demands of him. And he would have responsibilities to face. The thought made him restless.

"I should go," he said, turning to pack up his belongings.

"Yes," she agreed quietly. She stood with her back to him until she heard his briefcase snap closed, then went to the door to open it.

"Hannah," he said gently, waiting until she looked at him. "I don't want to fight with you."

Hannah sighed. "I don't want to fight, either."

"We can work this out," he assured her.

"Can we? I'm not even sure what 'this' is." She sounded so hopeless that he wanted to hold her and give her comfort and reassurance in the only way he knew how. But he couldn't give her the one thing she wanted so desperately—a guarantee that he would stay in her life permanently. For some reason, that realization left him feeling empty and sad tonight.

"We have to," he said simply, "because you're not getting rid of me no matter how hard you try."

That, at least, brought a small smile to her face. "Remember, dinner tomorrow night," he said, dropping a soft kiss on her forehead before he left.

Hannah couldn't believe how quickly she had become an integral part of Jordan's life. She went to dinner with him the following night and then the night after that they had carry-out Chinese food in his office and a tour of the plant for Kevin. Hannah had worried about the dinner with Jordan's customers, but it was relaxed and friendly, and Jordan made it clear by the way he solicitously tended to Hannah that she was more than a mere date.

She couldn't believe that he was the same man she had known so long ago. He acted like...a man in love.

Her heart lurched at the prospect, but her reason warned her not to go spinning dreams out of gossamer. Still, for the first time she dared to hope.

Now it was Friday morning, and Jordan had left with Kevin on his motorcycle for Kevin's class picnic. Hannah was dropping off some personnel reports to the library before driving to the park in her car.

"You look sporty," Jessie told her, taking in Hannah's brown pants and black blouse with a white lace collar. "Going somewhere exciting with the Italian suit?"

Hannah rolled her eyes. "My son's first-grade picnic. More excitement than one sane person can handle with all that Kool-Aid and running and screaming."

"You're taking the Italian suit there?" Jessie asked in amazement. "What are you trying to do, drive him away?"

Hannah realized that when Jordan came back into her

life, driving him away had certainly been her objective. But even her sharp tongue and the problems of a fatherless six-year-old boy hadn't accomplished that. Now she didn't want him to leave.

"Kevin asked him to be his surrogate father," Hannah said.

"Wow." Jessie's eyes widened. "Does this guy have a brother?"

"Two, but they're both married." Hannah couldn't help grinning at Jessie's wonderstruck expression.

"Damn. A man like that's so good he should be shared."

Hannah laughed. "That sounds like a page out of Claire Peterson's philosophy book."

"You watch her," Jessie warned. "That one fishes with dynamite."

"Warning taken," Hannah said, glancing at her watch. "I'd better get to the park before the kids dismantle Jordan's motorcycle and him along with it."

Hannah could hear the picnic when she was a block away. Either that, or there was a screaming contest going on nearby.

She parked, then walked across the grass, finding Jordan and Kevin immediately. They were holding court beside Jordan's motorcycle, which was parked under a tree near the curb. A crowd of boisterous six-year-old boys milled about them, obviously impressed with both machine and owner.

The expression on Kevin's face made Hannah stop and stare in the throes of the feeling mothers get when they realize that their child is truly happy. Because that was what Kevin was. His eyes shone, and his grin was genuine.

Hannah made her way to them, her mood dropping a notch when she saw Claire Peterson clutching Jordan's arm and trying to ask him a question over the din of the boys' voices. She was leaning close and peering into his face with the zeal of a woman checking price tags at a garage sale.

Hannah stood to the side until Kevin looked up and cried, "Mom! You made it!"

Jordan turned around immediately, his smile sudden and warm when he saw her.

"I was just going to get Jordan to help us with the barbecue grill," Claire interjected, her smile so wide it looked as if she was ready to devour him. She was wearing very short shorts and a halter top.

"I can help you with that, Claire," Hannah volunteered.

"No, no, you spend some time with your son," Claire insisted, pulling hard on Jordan's arm. With an apologetic shrug toward Hannah, he followed.

One of the first-graders leaned close to Kevin and whispered loudly, "I can see Mrs. Peterson's heinie!"

Hannah gave him a stern look, stopping whatever he was about to say next. He was right though. Two half moons of flesh bulged out below the frayed ends of Claire's cut-offs.

"Thank heavens you're here," a voice said at her elbow, and Hannah turned to see one of the other mothers, Eleanor Spurgeon.

"Why?" Hannah asked. "Are the kids taking over?"

"Not the kids. It's Claire. She nearly spilled out of that top when she leaned over the motorcycle."

Hannah sighed. Jessie had been right. Claire fished with dynamite. She couldn't help but feel an uncomfortable twinge of jealousy as she remembered how Jordan had left her seven years ago.

"I could use some help with the wheelbarrow race," Eleanor said. "Are you game?"

"Sure." Hannah glanced toward the barbecue grills as she followed Eleanor. Claire was bending over a grill, blowing on a thin stream of smoke trickling up from the coals. Jordan stood beside her, looking...stoic, she decided. He glanced up, caught her eye and mouthed, *Help.*

Hannah gave him a helpless shake of her head, sure it would take a couple of Chippendale strippers proffering engagement rings—or hotel keys—to pry Claire away from Jordan now.

Eleanor clapped her hands and shouted, managing to round up most of the first-graders for the contest. Hannah went after the rest, collaring three girls chasing a squirrel up a tree.

The kids chose partners, and then Eleanor explained the race to them. One child would hold the other by the ankles, and the pair would race to a line several yards away.

Hannah took the can of orange spray paint, the kind that utility workers used to mark underground lines, and walked away, stopping to spray the line that Eleanor had already laid out with string and two stakes. She removed the stakes and string and stood, shading her eyes as she looked back at the group of kids.

There, in the midst of them, was Claire, bending down toward Jordan who was sitting on the grass tying his sneaker. Hannah walked back to the group in time to hear Claire say, "Come on, Jordan. Just grab my ankles. This'll be fun."

Jordan looked nearly panicked, and Hannah couldn't blame him. Claire upside down in that outfit was likely to get them all arrested.

"I don't think so," Jordan said quickly, obviously looking around for Hannah.

"All right, then," Claire called cheerfully. "I'll hold your ankles." Before Jordan could move, she dove at him like a sea gull after clams, grasping his ankles and trying to haul them upward from behind.

She nearly succeeded, but Jordan wasn't cooperating, and his weight proved to be too much for her. Claire sank down on the ground in defeat, fanning herself.

"You have the sexiest legs," she purred. "I just get goose bumps."

Hannah stifled a laugh and trotted back to the finish line to determine the winners. Eleanor blew a whistle, and fifteen pairs of wriggling arms and legs came barreling toward

Hannah. Keeping most of her attention on the contestants, Hannah managed to watch Jordan from the corner of her eye as Claire herded him back toward the grills.

After first-, second- and third-place winners were awarded prizes of soap bubble bottles with wands, Eleanor nudged Hannah.

"Are you going to rescue your friend or not?"

Hannah glanced again at the grills where Claire was giggling as she tried to tie an apron around Jordan's waist.

"He deserves a dose of Claire," she said, realizing that her jealousy had disappeared as soon as she realized that Jordan wasn't the least bit interested in the other woman.

"Well, I sure hope you do something before she ties him to the hood of her car and takes him home to mount over the fireplace," Eleanor said.

Hannah turned back to the next game, the three-legged race.

"Want to be my partner?" Kevin asked another boy who was smaller than most of the kids and obviously a loner.

The boy nodded, brightening, and Hannah smiled at them.

Apparently Kevin's surrogate father had boosted his confidence. As far as she could tell, none of the other kids had teased him or shunned him today. Jordan and the motorcycle had done the trick.

At that, she felt guilty about abandoning Jordan to Claire, and as soon as the race was over, she made her way to the grills.

"Sorry, Claire," she said sweetly, "but I need to borrow Jordan."

Claire's face fell in disappointment, and Jordan came away with Hannah so quickly that Hannah wondered if he'd left sneaker tread marks on the grass.

"About time," he growled into her ear.

"Don't tell me the Great Bachelor was having difficulty handling a woman," she said with mock surprise.

"That's no woman," he told her. "That's a barracuda. And what took you so long, anyway?"

"I thought you might be enjoying yourself," she said.

"What?" He stopped in his tracks and looked at her as if she was certainly daft. "Why on earth would you think I was enjoying myself?"

Hannah studied his handsome face. He looked genuinely surprised. She gave a half smile.

"Because she's a woman, and you're—"

"The Great Bachelor," he finished for her wryly. "Hannah, I'm not about to throw you over for anyone else, and you might as well get used to it."

She grinned in spite of her misgivings. He looked so annoyed with her.

"Is that right?" she said.

"Yes, that's right," he said, ruffling her hair. "Now, come on. I can't wait to get you in the water balloon toss contest."

It was late afternoon when Jordan and Hannah returned to Jordan's apartment. Kevin had gone to a movie matinee with Eleanor's son and two other friends.

Jordan's jeans and shirt were soaked and dirty from the water balloon toss and the egg toss, and as soon as they were inside he began to strip them off.

Hannah felt herself blushing, but she made no move to leave the living room. In fact, she watched him with avid interest.

Jordan looked up as he pulled off his jeans and gave her a slow grin.

"Enjoying yourself?" he asked.

"Yes," she said frankly, beginning to smile herself. "You have the sexiest legs," she twittered, parodying Claire. "I just get goose bumps."

"I'll give you goose bumps," he threatened with a mock growl.

Jordan walked to her slowly, his eyes ablaze with undisguised hunger. She began to tremble inside with the need he could make her feel with just a look.

"I'm going to take a shower," he drawled slowly. "Want to join me?"

Hannah laced her fingers behind his neck when he was close enough and drew down his head for a kiss.

"I shouldn't," she sighed.

"Because you can't let it lead to anything more?" he asked, pulling back far enough to study her face.

"Please, Jordan. This is hard for me, too." She abruptly released him and turned away.

Jordan felt a restless frustration rise within him. He wanted to hold her and kiss her. He wanted her beside him in bed. He wanted to know that she would be coming home to him every night.

What he wanted didn't make sense to him. But there it was. The thought of spending the rest or his life with her didn't panic him. He had no desire to run for the door.

It seemed so long ago now that he had gloated over his freedom to come and go as he pleased. For all of his adult years he had shunned any commitment that would tie him to another person, that would add any restrictions to his life. And now, in a matter of days—of hours even—he found that particular freedom from commitment tiring. The ability to come and go at will was a restriction in itself, because it gave nothing in return.

Now he felt like he owned the world.

It was because he had a son.

He had a son, and he wanted all the things that went with that. The whole package.

He said Hannah's name softly, and something in the tone made her look at him again.

"Hannah, I've been thinking…"

She waited, trying to decipher the expression on his face. He looked uncomfortable, and for a moment she froze, afraid that he was about to leave her for good.

"I'm not very good at this," he said, trying to smile and

not succeeding. He abruptly turned his back on her and took a deep breath. "What I'm trying to say is..."

He turned around to face her again and apparently found that he couldn't say it after all.

"Jordan! You're scaring me. What is it?"

"I'm sorry," he said, immediately taking her into his arms and caressing her hair with one hand. "I never want to scare you. What I was wondering is...I mean, would you...would you want to get married? To me?" he added as if she might think he had someone else in mind.

Hannah was dumbstruck. She stared at him with wide, disbelieving eyes.

"What did you say?"

"I know what I said," he told her urgently. "But I think I'm ready for marriage. We'd be good together. And then there's Kevin. You know how I feel about him."

"Married?" she breathed. "Do you really mean it?"

"Yes, of course I mean it. You know me well enough, Hannah, to realize that I wouldn't say it otherwise. I told you once that I don't play games. This isn't some trick to get you into bed with me." He suddenly grinned. "Although I wouldn't be at all opposed to getting you into bed again, that is if your high principles will let you make love to your fiancé."

"Oh, Jordan," she said, totally lost for words. "I don't know what to say."

"Well, you could start with 'Yes, I think I might be so inclined, Jordan' or 'Yes, it's fine with me, Jordan.' Hannah, please say yes and don't look at me like you think I might be losing my mind."

"Yes," she said, suddenly unsure whether to laugh or cry. "Yes," she said again, feeling tears well in her eyes even as she began to laugh. "And I *do* think you're losing your mind. You've never wanted marriage, Jordan."

"True," he admitted, his hands cupping her face. "But I do now. Of that I'm sure." He grinned at her and crooked one finger tantalizingly. "Have you ever showered with your fiancé before, Hannah?"

No, she hadn't, but it was a wonderfully wicked idea, and she stripped as he led her toward the bathroom.

She knew that she was in a state of shock at the moment. But she had no time to dwell on it, because Jordan had pulled her into the bathroom and was reaching behind himself to turn on the shower while he used his other hand to caress her naked back. His mouth brushed hers softly, and then, with a groan, he deepened the kiss until Hannah grew dizzy with the sensations racing through her.

The volatile combination of his touch and his unexpected marriage proposal was turning her knees to jelly, and she clutched at his shoulders.

"Jordan," she breathed hoarsely. She opened her eyes to find him smiling at her, his eyes filled with beguiling promises. She suddenly wanted to feel him inside her, touching her where no one else had. As if reading her thoughts, his face turned serious. Cupping her chin in one hand, he brushed her lips with his again.

"Lovely lady," he whispered hoarsely, "do you know how much I want you right now?"

Hannah swallowed, unable to speak. He was so handsome that he took her breath away. His body with its chiseled muscles and flat planes made her burn with lust for him, but what she saw in his sky blue eyes was a heaven and a haven, the promise of everything she'd ever wanted.

She squealed in surprise as he suddenly scooped her up in his arms and gently carried her into the shower. Hannah laughed and clung to his neck as the warm spray pelted her.

Jordan set her on her feet under the water and began a slow, torturous exploration of her body with his mouth and fingers. Combined with the warm spray, his touch had her moaning in seconds. But still he pleasured her, his hands finding her most sensitive places, stroking and teasing until she nearly sobbed with her need for him.

He brought her close to him then so that she was pressed against his hard male flesh, then lifted her with his hands on her hips and entered her in one smooth thrust.

Hannah cried out and wrapped her legs around him, pressing her mouth against his shoulder in a spasm of desire. It was as if his marriage proposal had leveled the last barrier in her heart.

No one else could ever make her feel like this, whether in a shower or a bed or anyplace else on earth. It was Jordan she wanted, had always wanted.

The ripples of pleasure overwhelmed her, and she heard herself say his name with all of her love invested in it.

"Yes, sweetheart," he groaned, answering her with his body, his own pleasure taking his breath away.

When they had recovered and leaned against each other, murmuring soft endearments, Hannah felt languid and as satisfied as a cat basking in the sun.

She arched her back and smiled up at Jordan as he began to carefully and sensually soap her body. He smiled back, and incredibly the heat began to build between them again.

Ten

Hannah sat stretched out on the grass in the shade, staring up at Esther's new house. The roof sheathing had just been completed, and everyone was taking a break.

She glanced over at Jordan, sitting two feet away, and grinned. He lowered the bottle of beer he had been sipping and grinned back. She couldn't believe that only the night before he had asked her to marry him.

Esther set the tray of plastic glasses down on the picnic table with a bang and looked from Jordan to Hannah, her hands on her hips.

"Are you two going to tell me what's going on?" she demanded. "I can pry it out of you, you know."

Jordan laughed. "Honestly, Esther, how could we keep a secret from you?"

She frowned at him. "A good-looking sucker like you can probably keep a lot of secrets, but you ain't gonna keep them from me for long. *I'm*—what's that word?—impervious to your charms. Yeah, I got charms of my own."

Hannah couldn't hold back her laughter.

"Esther, you're one of a kind," she said.

"Yeah, that's me," Esther grunted. "If I was any more charming, I'd be illegal. Now, everybody eat these cookies or I'll throw 'em to the hogs."

"Ma, we don't have hogs," Ronnie said reasonably.

"Don't push me, Ronnie, or I'll be buying some and giving all your food to them."

Hannah exchanged another glance with Jordan. They hadn't told Kevin yet about their engagement, and they didn't want to make any announcements before he knew.

"All right," John said, pushing to his feet. "Who's ready to do some roofing?"

"I wouldn't let Jordan up there," Jake advised him slowly. "I don't think his mind's on building today. Same goes for Hannah."

"Yeah," John said, grinning. "It would be just like the two of them to fall off the roof today."

"Like they're thinking of something else," Jake hinted again, lifting his brows as he looked at Jordan.

Jordan grinned and gave Jake a casual punch on the arm.

"Rattle on all you want," he said cheerfully. "You're not bothering me."

"So when did he stop blabbing everything he knows?" John asked Jake plaintively.

"When he turned twelve," Jake said wryly. He gave Hannah an innocent look. "Come on, Hannah. What's with you two?"

Hannah laughed. "Beats me. Must be something in the water."

Jordan's brothers finally gave up their quest for information and climbed up to the roof. Ronnie helped them while Hannah and Jordan worked on the cornices from atop tall stepladders.

It was obvious that both of Jordan's brothers *and* Ronnie *and* Esther were eavesdropping for everything they were worth, so Jordan and Hannah didn't talk except to request a tool. Even then, four heads tilted in their direction at the slightest hint of conversation.

Hannah was despairing of ever getting Jordan alone again by the end of the day. Kevin, oblivious to the intrigue going on around him, had chatted happily and borrowed Ronnie's old bicycle to ride around the driveway. When it was time for him to go to bed, he asked both Hannah and Jordan to tuck him in.

Hannah sat on the edge of his bed and read him a story, a tradition he loved even though he could read by himself now. Then Jordan smiled and said, "Close your eyes."

"Sweet sleep," Kevin answered, a tired smile lighting his face.

"Dream a dream," Hannah said.

"For me to keep," Kevin finished. His eyes drifted closed as he squeezed Hannah's hand. "Wow, this is so great..." His voice trailed off, and Hannah leaned down to kiss his forehead, that sweet little-boy forehead with a spill of silky hair. He was such an uncomplicated boy. At this age, his heart was on his sleeve, and everything was new and wonderful to him.

Hannah stood and nodded her head toward the door. Jordan followed her in the dark, his hand finding her waist and sliding down to cup her hip. They made their way through the trailer to the front door, both of them laughing softly like teenagers.

The TV was on in Esther's bedroom, and Hannah held one finger to her lips and did an exaggerated tiptoe past her door. Jordan was right behind her, teasing her by tickling her ribs with two fingers until she gave a low squeal and darted out the front door.

The air was balmy and the night sky filled with so many stars that it glowed like a living, shimmering swath of silk.

Esther's porch light was on, but the orange bulb, purported to keep bugs away, gave only a soft puddle of illumination.

Hannah sat on the concrete step and made room for Jordan. He stood for a moment breathing in the fresh air, then dropped down beside her, his hip and leg tight against hers. He swung one hand down through the dewy grass and plucked up a stalk of the sage that Esther planted and that now ran riot next to the trailer.

"Smell that," he said, holding it out to Hannah.

It was pungent and tangy, its first blooms ready to form.

"You like plants, don't you?" he asked lazily. "I was thinking maybe we should get a place in the country where we could go on weekends. Kevin could keep a horse there if he wanted and ride a dirt bike."

Hannah studied his face in the pale light. She had never thought that he could be like this. That she could be like this.

"I should tell you," she said softly, "that I want to have children."

He smiled. "More children. Hannah, don't you think it's time you told me the truth?"

"The truth?" she repeated blankly. She didn't understand what he meant.

Jordan leaned back against the trailer, shaking his head. She was still so determined that he not know. "Hannah," he began, trailing his hand in the sage again. His finger caught on something, and he lifted it, catching a soft glint of metal. He didn't finish what he had been about to say as he realized what he was holding.

"My locket!" Hannah cried, reaching immediately for it. "Oh, Jordan, I thought I'd never see it again."

He watched as she carefully opened the clasp and gently held it up to the light. She traced her finger lovingly over the tiny photo inside.

"I don't have another copy of this picture," she explained. "And this is the only one of Kevin with his real mother. I meant to have a copy made, but..." She shrugged, relieved just to have this one back.

"Kevin's real mother," he repeated, his face gone expressionless.

"My sister, Marybeth," Hannah said.

"Kevin isn't your son?"

She shook her head. "I thought you knew. I guess I just assumed that everyone knew. Marybeth died shortly after he was born. That was why I left my job at McClennon Industries—she got pregnant, and there was no one to take care of her."

"What about Kevin's father?" he asked, and she realized that what she saw on his face was shock.

"Marybeth wasn't even sure who he was," she said slowly, trying to understand why he looked the way he did, why Kevin's parentage came as such a surprise. "I got a job near her to help out, and when she died I was given custody. I came back here, because this felt more like home to me." She had been watching his face with growing alarm, because something was obviously wrong.

"Jordan, what is it?" she asked suddenly. "Why is it so surprising to you that Kevin is my sister's child? Did you think he was biologically mine?"

She still didn't understand why that fact would be such a revelation to him. She frowned. But, if he had thought that, why had he never asked her who Kevin's father was?

And then she understood. She understood it all.

"Oh…" she said softly, the color draining from her face. "Oh. You thought…" She couldn't finish the sentence.

Jordan finally spoke, his voice low and still incredulous.

"For God's sake, Hannah, how could I *not* think that? The timing was right, and you seemed so…angry to see me again. And so protective of Kevin. What man wouldn't wonder?"

It all made sense to her now. Horrible, painful sense.

He had wanted to be with his son. Not her. But the son he thought he had fathered.

And now that he knew the truth…

Hannah stood up quickly, fumbling for the door.

"Hannah, wait! We have to talk." He reached for her

arm, but she wrenched it away as if it hurt to have him touch her.

"I'm sorry," she said, her eyes wide with pain. "I'm sorry I put you through all of this. You can go back to your life now, Jordan. Really. I understand."

"Hannah, don't send me away. Please. You don't understand."

"Don't try to put a pretty face on your goodbyes this time, Jordan," she said, trying very hard not to cry—yet. "Let's make it clean and fast. I absolve you of all responsibility for me or Kevin. He is absolutely not your child in any way whatsoever. You can go your own way now, Jordan. Back to the life you really want. And, please..." Her voice wavered, but she took a deep breath. "Please don't try to see us again."

"Hannah," he said, feeling more helpless than he ever had in his life. But she was already inside, and the lock turned with a hollow sound of finality.

Hannah resolutely kept her eyes on her apartment building door as she passed the flower boxes out front. Even though a month had passed since she discovered the real reason Jordan wanted to marry her, she still nearly burst into tears each time she looked at the pansies.

Hannah had left Esther's trailer with Kevin late the night Jordan found the locket, borrowing Esther's aged VW to drive home. She'd told Esther what had happened, leaving out most of the details and concluding that it had been a bad mistake for both her and Jordan to get involved.

Esther had listened and then had hugged Hannah hard, telling her to go ahead and take the car.

Ronnie and one of his friends had picked up the car the next day. Ronnie was sad for her and awkwardly at a loss for words. Hannah had told him that it was for the best, anyway.

It was Kevin who worried her the most. She could see that he was trying hard not to cry when she told him that

Jordan wouldn't be around them any longer. It was no-body's fault, she'd said. These things sometimes happened with adults.

"Then I'm never gonna grow up," Kevin said with the absolute certainty of a hurt six-year-old. "You can't trust grown-ups."

He was right, Hannah thought. You couldn't trust grown-ups, especially where your heart was involved.

Jordan had called twice in the preceding month, and both times Hannah had hung up the phone the instant she heard his voice. She was done with Jordan McClennon, no matter how much it hurt to admit it.

It was a hot Saturday morning in early July when Hannah came back from the laundromat to find Esther's VW parked at the curb in front of her apartment.

Hannah held the basket of clean, folded clothes to one side and leaned down to look in the passenger side.

"Are you lost?" she asked, trying to sound cheerful.

Esther bounced out of the car immediately.

"There you are! I was hoping I didn't come all this way for nothing."

"Come on in," Hannah said, leading the way to the apartment and trying hard not to ask exactly why Esther had come all this way.

"Where's Kevin?" Esther asked when they were in the door.

Hannah set the laundry basket down by the breakfast bar.

"He's swimming at a friend's house. Esther, is something wrong?"

"Oh, my goodness, no. Everything's fine." Esther was looking around the apartment and definitely fidgeting.

"Would you like something to drink?" Hannah asked.

"Yes. Yes, I would. Do you have any lemonade?"

"Yes, I mixed up a pitcher last night." Hannah was on her way to the refrigerator when Esther stopped her.

"No, no, I don't think it's lemonade I want after all. Grape soda. That's it. Do you have any grape soda?"

Hannah frowned. "No. But I've got orange soda."

"No, no. Has to be grape. I just got me a hankering for some grape soda. That's it."

Hannah sighed. "Well, we could go out for one."

Esther was already heading for the door. "Great! I could use a stretch of the legs."

"Well, I thought we could drive to the supermarket," Hannah said as she locked the door. "There's one about a mile from here."

"Oh, I'm just so tired of sitting in a car," Esther said. "Isn't there someplace we could walk to?"

"I suppose we could walk to Bettleman's if that's what you want to do."

"Sounds great. Let's go."

Esther was already marching off in the direction of Bettleman's, and Hannah was so undone by her precipitous visit that she didn't stop to wonder how Esther knew which way to go.

Esther made no small talk along the way, and Hannah kept quiet, unable to stop wondering what this was all about. She thought that if it concerned Jordan, then Esther was waiting an unusually long time to broach the subject.

Bettleman's was cool and dark after the intensely bright heat of the city sidewalk, and Hannah stopped a moment to let her eyes adjust.

"You go get the soda, and I'll just browse through the vegetables," Esther suggested, waving her hand at Hannah dismissively.

Whatever Esther had on her mind, Hannah couldn't begin to fathom it. Shaking her head, she headed for the soda aisle.

She turned the corner and found herself face-to-face with Jordan. For a moment she couldn't move or speak. The blood pounded in her head, and she nearly groaned with the hard realization that she still loved him. She might still be angry, but it hadn't killed the love she felt.

"Before you say anything," he said quickly, reaching

for her arm and then changing his mind, ''don't blame Esther.''

''Fine,'' she said shortly. ''I'll blame you.'' She started to turn away but found she didn't want to leave. Just seeing him was like a long, cool drink in the middle of the desert. She stood and stared.

''Hannah, I need to say something to you. I know you don't want to hear it, but I'm going to say it, anyway. And maybe then you'll at least talk to me again.''

''We've said everything that needs to be said,'' she told him, suddenly weary from her internal war with her feelings for him.

''No, we haven't.'' His eyes searched her face. ''You never told me you love me.''

Hannah gave a bitter laugh. ''Is that it? You want the final proof of just how irresistible you are?''

''No,'' he said sharply. ''I want something to build a marriage on.''

''Oh, here's a good foundation,'' she said. ''A boy who adores you but turns out not to be your own flesh and blood, after all and a woman who's hopelessly in love with you. You could work wonders with that.''

He ignored her sarcasm.

''You do love me, don't you?''

Hannah gave up the fight. What did it matter now?

''What difference does it make? Marriage is a trap for you, a cage. You'd hate it.''

''Don't you understand?'' he demanded, forgetting his qualms about touching her as his fingers closed on her shoulders. ''What I'm in now is the cage. A cage in hell. Don't you know what it's like to not be able to sleep or work because you've realized how alone you are? Because the person who can make you laugh and make you angry and make you glad you're alive doesn't want you anymore?''

She still didn't believe him.

"It's a phase," she said, tears filling her eyes because she was still suffering in that particular phase herself.

"Damn it, Hannah, I want to marry you! I thought I was seeing you because of Kevin, because he was my son. And then when I found out he's not— Don't you see? It doesn't matter that he's not my son! I miss him and I miss you. I want us to be together. I don't want to go on like this anymore."

Hannah was nearly crying now.

"It wouldn't work, Jordan. It just wouldn't work." He didn't love her. He hadn't said the words, and he never would. She couldn't marry him without his love.

She pulled away from his grip and headed blindly for the door, tears spilling down her cheeks. Two elderly women shoppers stepped aside for her, obviously curious. Calvin the stock boy began a pompous announcement on the public address system about a special on canned peaches.

Hannah had forgotten about Esther and frankly didn't care at the moment. She just had to get away from Jordan.

The stock boy's announcement ended in mid-sentence, and Hannah stopped when she heard Jordan's voice booming through the store.

"Hannah Brewster, I love you, and if you walk out of here now, I swear I'll be back here every Saturday, and I'll make this same announcement until you say you'll marry me."

She turned and wiped her eyes, seeing him at the service counter beside the produce, still holding the microphone to his lips. A stunned stock boy stood beside him. Esther was three feet away, squeezing a tomato in each hand.

"Hannah," he said into the microphone again, "will you *please* marry me?"

She didn't trust herself to speak, so she met his eyes and slowly nodded yes. *Yes!*

Jordan began to smile, a smile that turned into a grin. He put down the microphone and ran toward her as Esther threw down the tomatoes and began to applaud. Leslie at checkout was clapping as well, and so were the two shoppers.

"Hannah, Hannah," he murmured, pulling her into his arms and raining kisses on her face. "I never knew it would be like this."

"What?" she teased him, still wiping away tears.

"Love," he said. "I didn't know it would turn me inside out. Hannah, I've barely survived."

He sounded so aggrieved that she laughed.

"You were a great bachelor," she told him, kissing him hard.

"Maybe so," he said, leaning back to look at her face and smiling. "But I'm going to make an even better husband."

Epilogue

Jordan and Hannah were married in August in an outdoor ceremony at Esther's new house. The house had been finished, or nearly so, and in anticipation of the wedding, Esther had installed a wooden arch near the woods and planted honeysuckle that ran rampant up and over it.

The weather was perfect, and the woods made a verdant backdrop for the wedding couple as they took their vows in the cool shade of the honeysuckle.

Neither had wanted a large wedding, but the guests made up for their small numbers with enthusiasm.

Kevin served as best man for his new father, and Esther couldn't stop grinning as she stood proudly beside Hannah as matron of honor.

"You're beautiful," Jordan said to Hannah as she came to stand beside him in her white gown. Instead of a headpiece, she had chosen a white hat that Jake's wife, Laura, made for her. White veiling wrapped around the hat and tied in a bow in the back.

Smiling, Hannah took Jordan's hand.

"You're beautiful, too," she said, and she meant it. He was the most handsome man she had ever known in her life. And she could still hardly believe that he really wanted to marry her.

But he did. She believed him now.

Jordan's family had turned out in force: John and Rachel with their two sons, David and his baby brother, Michael; Jake and Laura, who was only now beginning to show signs of her pregnancy, with their daughter, Molly; and Jordan's mother, Elizabeth, who had warmly welcomed Hannah into the family.

Blessed was how Elizabeth said she felt, and Hannah felt that way, too. She had never had much of a family herself, and Jordan's happy, loving clan was one of the newest riches of her life.

Jordan had had a somewhat traditional bachelor's party the night before the wedding, and Ronnie had sheepishly confided the details to his mother, who passed them along to Hannah.

He said it wasn't the usual rowdy celebration. Jordan and his brothers had drunk only soda, and they had raised their glasses at the end of the evening to toast their wives and Jordan's bride-to-be.

According to Ronnie, the only shenanigans occurred when Jordan pulled out a kazoo and reminded his brothers of their promise if Jordan ever got married. John had said he would dance naked around the St. Jude statue, and Jake had said he would play the kazoo.

Ronnie wouldn't give any more details about that particular episode, but he kept grinning.

As the wedding ceremony concluded, Jordan took his bride in his arms and kissed her long and hard to the delight of their guests.

But only Hannah heard him whisper, "Dream a dream." And she answered in kind. "For me to keep."

They turned and walked down the path and into their new life together.

Esther dabbed at her eyes and followed, stopping at the edge of her new flower garden just long enough to take a single rose from her bouquet and drop it in front of the cement garden elf that Ronnie had moved there from the diner.

"Well done, old boy," she whispered.

*   *   *   *   *

FANTASTIC NEWS!

For all you devoted Diana Palmer fans
Silhouette Books is pleased to bring you
a brand-new novel and short story by one of the
top ten romance writers in America

"Nobody tops Diana Palmer...I love her stories."
—*New York Times* bestselling author
Jayne Ann Krentz

**Diana Palmer has written another thrilling desire.
Man of the Month Ramon Cortero was a talented
surgeon, existing only for his work—until the
night he saved nurse Noreen Kensington's life. But
their stormy past makes this romance a challenge!**

THE PATIENT NURSE
Silhouette Desire
October 1997

And in November Diana Palmer adds to the
Long, Tall Texans series with *CHRISTMAS COWBOY*, in
LONE STAR CHRISTMAS, a fabulous new holiday
keepsake collection by talented authors Diana Palmer
and Joan Johnston. Their heroes are seductive,
shameless and irresistible—and these Texans are
experts at sneaking kisses under the mistletoe! So get
ready for a sizzling holiday season....

Only from ▼™ *Silhouette*®

EXTRA***EXTRA***EXTRA
Temptation, Texas, advertises for women.

Salt-of-the-earth bachelors in search of
Mrs. Happily-ever-after. Read what the men of the
town have to say about their search:

Harley Kerr: I've lived my whole life in Temptation, Texas,
and I don't know what this foolish business about needing
women is all about. I've already done the wedded-bliss thing
once, and I'd rather wrestle a Texas rattler than walk down
the aisle again! **(MARRY ME, COWBOY, SD#1084, 7/97)**

Hank Braden: Women! I love 'em! The shape of 'em, the feel
of 'em, the scent of 'em. But I don't expect to be getting
permanently attached to any of them! I've got too many wild
oats to sow to be contemplating marriage!
(A LITTLE TEXAS TWO-STEP, SD#1090, 8/97)

Cody Fipes: When I suggested advertising for women, it
wasn't for *me!* There's only ever been one woman for me....
Besides, with all these new folks moving into Temptation,
I've got too much to do as sheriff to spend time investigating
a wife! **(LONE STAR KIND OF MAN, SD#1096, 9/97)**

**Starting in July from Silhouette Desire and Peggy Moreland,
three tales about love—and trouble—in Texas!**

**TROUBLE IN TEXAS.... When Temptation beckons,
three rugged cowboys lose their hearts.**

Available wherever Silhouette books are sold.

Look us up on-line at: http://www.romance.net   TROUB

ATTENTION
ALL JOAN JOHNSTON FANS!

Silhouette Books is pleased to bring you two brand-new additions to the #1 bestselling Hawk's Way series—the novel you've all been waiting for and a short story....

"Joan Johnston does contemporary westerns to perfection." —*Publishers Weekly*

Remember those Whitelaws of Texas from Joan Johnston's HAWK'S WAY series? Jewel Whitelaw is all grown up and is about to introduce Mac Macready to the wonders of passion! You see, Mac is a virgin...and it's going to be one long, hot summer....

HAWK'S WAY
THE VIRGIN GROOM
August 1997

And in November don't miss Rolleen Whitelaw's love story, *A HAWK'S WAY CHRISTMAS*, in **LONE STAR CHRISTMAS**, a fabulous new holiday keepsake collection by talented authors Joan Johnston and Diana Palmer. Their heroes are seductive, shameless and irresistible—and these Texans are experts in sneaking kisses under the mistletoe! So get ready for a sizzling holiday season....

Only from

They called her the

Champagne Girl

Catherine: Underneath the effervescent, carefree and bubbly
facade there was a depth to which few
had access.

Matt: The older stepbrother she inherited with her
mother's second marriage, Matt continually
complicated things. It seemed to Catherine that
she would make plans only to have Matt foul
them up.

With the perfect job waiting in New York City, only one thing
would be able to keep her on a dusty cattle ranch: something
she thought she could never have—the love of the sexiest
cowboy in the Lone Star state.

by bestselling author

DIANA PALMER

Available in September 1997 at your favorite retail outlet.

 MIRA The brightest star in women's fiction   MDP8

Look us up on-line at: http://www.romance.net